MW00326100

YARN OF DESTINY

Yarn Of Destiny

REBEKAH NANCE

Copyright © 2021 by

All rights reserved. No part of this book may be reproduced in any
manner whatsoever without written permission except in the case
of brief quotations embodied in critical articles and reviews.

First Printing, 2021

To My True Love, Sierra V.: Thank you for being the best partner I could've ever asked for. I love you so much.

To My Parents: I'll always love you.

- R.N.

Spells and their meanings:

Excuse Me – the spell caster passes by people without question

Please and thank you - get someone to do something for the spell caster without question

Abracadabra - make the spell caster and anyone who touches them impervious to anything

Alakazam - make the spell caster walk faster

Hocus Pocus - make someone make sense in what they are trying to say

Sleight of Hand - make something from someone's hand disappear and reappear into the spell caster's or vice versa

Lightning Basalt – make a lightning bolt strike a person dead, only to be used under extreme circumstances, such as battle

Dissolve Hinge – dissolve a door's hinges to make the doorway passable

Elemental Rain – make the elements (earth, wind, fire, water) rain down like, well, rain. Can be used in battle.

Purity of Strength – make someone with a pure heart and pure intentions stronger than they normally are

Magical Object:

Ball Of Yarn

When it runs out, so does the magic of the spell caster, and each must go on a quest to find the girl who spins the magic yarn to get more magic. Balls of yarn may be made into sweaters, socks, etc., but must be used sparingly, and those made objects are magic, but the magic fades faster than with the ball of yarn itself. Each spell caster gets a twelve-foot-long ball of yarn from the time they are ten years old and must carry it with them wherever they go. Each time a spell is cast, an inch of yarn shimmers and fades to a pale color version of the favorite color of the spell caster, thus needing to be snipped from the ball, and it becomes regular everyday yarn.

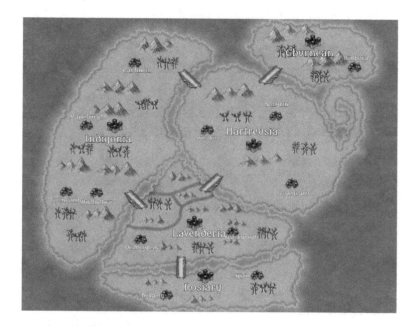

Planet Gnypso's History
This planet is similar to Earth.
Year Lands Founded: 2864
Countries:

- Eburnean (Castle Morrison)
- Indigonia (Castle Cantrell)
- Hartreusia (Castle Atteberry)
- Lavenderia (Castle Arellano)

• Rosiary (Castle Villareal)

Eburnean – Smallest of the five countries, Eburnean houses Castle Morrison, and they are closest in terms of allyship to Hartreusia.

Indigonia – Indigonia houses Castle Cantrell and are farthest in terms of allyship to Hartreusia.

Hartreusia – Main country, home of Castle Atteberry.

Lavenderia – Biggest of the five countries, Lavenderia houses Castle Arellano and is home to Luana's extended family.

Rosiary – Second smallest of the five countries, Rosiary is home to Castle Villareal and is where Nona is from.

Destinism's Ten Decrees Specifically For Magic Folk (Spell Casters)

1. In order to use magic, one must respect magic.
2. One shall not use magic unless necessary.
3. Healing crystals can only be used for major injuries and illnesses.
4. When using up one's ball of yarn, use it sparingly.
5. With magic, one cannot use it on live animals.
6. One may use magic for teaching others magic.
7. One may use magic for cooking, but only once a month.
8. One must not waste magic on trivial things.
9. Magic is not a toy and should not be treated as such.
10. The yarn is mightier than the pen, which is mightier than the sword.

Destinism's Ten Decrees For All Folk

1. One shall not marry a spell caster if one is not a spell caster.
2. One shall not steal a spell caster's ball of yarn.
3. One shall make peace with all spell casters.
4. When on The Quest, the dangers of it shall remain unknown, and no one is allowed to let the questers know what the dangers are going

to be.

    5. One shall not interfere with a spell caster's magic doing.

    6. Trades should be fair and binding.

    7. Ladies must wear attire appropriate for their status.

    8. Gentlemen must wear attire appropriate for their status.

    9. Non-binary folk, genderfluid folk, agender folk, etc, may wear attire of their choosing, but must be appropriate for their status.

    10. Pronouns must be used properly, and may not be changed unless necessary, no matter how cross you are at the person.

~ One ~

In all honesty, Luana did not understand how she had ended up in such a mess.

One moment, she was on the quest with her best friend and lady-in-waiting, Nona, and her future queen consort. The next, she was tied up by the girl who spins the magic yarn.

But, to understand how Luana got into this debacle, we have to go back two weeks, to the beginning of this story:

The year is 2997, on the dwarf planet Gnypso in the Omnicron Nebula galaxy. There are five countries on Gnypso: Hartreusia, Rosiary, Lavenderia, Indigonia, and Eburnean.

This story, at its start, takes place in Hartreusia, specifically in Nahurin.

Hartreusia is ruled by King Carter, Queen Juniper, and their seventeen-year-old daughter, Princess Luana. King Carter Atteberry has green eyes, light ebony skin, and black hair, while Queen Juniper has red hair, brown eyes and light ebony skin. Princess Luana has brown eyes, red hair and light ebony skin, and her button nose is like her father's.

According to tradition, Luana must be married by the time she turns eighteen, and that is only a few months away. Her parents could not care less whether she married man or maiden, as long as whoever she chooses to marry is a royal.

But Luana would rather marry her confidante, best friend and lady-in-waiting, Nona Hamlett of Lippin in Rosiary.

However, because of the old ways, Luana cannot marry her best friend, and not just because Nona is not a royal; Nona is also a spell caster, and spell casters and royals are never allowed to marry, as it would clash with the bloodline. There has never been a spell caster that's a royal, and there's never been a royal that's a spell caster; Luana's ancestors made sure of that.

Now, Luana and Nona are out in the palace garden, in the fenced-in field, making flower crowns and talking with one another. Luana is wearing a simple short blue picnic dress with floral details, while Nona wears a simple green picnic dress, also with floral details.

Nona has fair skin, shoulder-length thick brown hair, hazel eyes, a round nose and pink lips.

Once the girls are finished making flower crowns, they lay side by side under a willow tree, their flower crowns on their heads.

"Nona?"

"Yes, Princess?"

"You don't have to call me that in private, you know."

"I mean it as a term of endearment. You know."

Luana sticks her tongue out at her confidante, and Nona returns the gesture.

"Tell me again how your magic works."

"Are you sure? With the limp I caused five years ago, I wouldn't want to bring back those painful memories for you."

"You will not. Besides, only *I* can control my memories. Please, Nona?" Luana asks, flipping onto her side and propping her head up on her hand to get a better look at her girlfriend.

"Well, as you know, yarn is the source of our magic. When our ball of yarn runs out, so, too, does our magic. Then we must go on a quest to find the girl who spins the magic yarn. No one knows where or who she even is, as the questers' and their companions' memories are wiped of the girl's location and her appearance. There are only ten known spells in the magic system, and, when a spell is said, an inch of yarn turns to a pale shade of the spell caster's favorite color, rendering it unusable. On our tenth birthday, we get a twelve-foot-long ball of yarn and we must carry it with us wherever we go, should we need to use our magic."

"What about the healing magic?"

"Luana, you know that healing magic faded out centuries ago, and only the spell where you get someone to do something for you without question can be used to heal, unless you use healing crystals. No one knows why healing magic faded out, only that one day it was there, and the next, it wasn't."

"Do you think healing crystals could heal my limp?"

"I don't believe so, Luana. What I did to you is untreatable."

Luana winces and puts a hand to her left hip.

"You alright?"

"It's just my leg pains again. We should be getting back. My aunt and uncle and little cousins are due to visit soon from Lavenderia, and my mother will expect me to look presentable at dinner."

Nona gets up, her flower crown slightly askew, and offers Luana a hand up.

"Come on. I'll help you get ready for dinner tonight."

"Thank you, Nona."

"You're welcome."

The two girls head back inside, and Nona can't help but notice Luana's limp has gotten worse over the past five years.

They head up to Luana's bedchamber, and Luana picks out a purple dress with bell sleeves.

"Nona, can we scrap the sleeves? They do make it so hard to eat, drink and be merry."

Nona nods, and takes a pair of fabric scissors and snips the sleeves from the dress, as it was a last-minute change. After that is done, Nona goes and gets Luana's dinner tiara, a golden tiara with pearls, diamonds, and tree branch accents.

After putting Luana's red hair in an intricate braided bun, Nona carefully places the tiara on Luana's head.

Luana stands up and places herself in front of the full-length mirror to get a good look at herself.

She turns around so Nona can have a glance.

"Well, how do I look?"

"Like a vision."

"Thank you, Nona. Come on. Let's get *you* ready now."

"If you insist, Luana. But you better not make us late for the dinner."

"I won't. You can borrow one of my dresses. We *are* the same size, after all."

Luana helps Nona step into a silver, long-sleeved dress that won't outshine her own dress, as is protocol.

After Nona's short brown locks have a slight curl to them, Nona and Luana head down to dinner. They are greeted by Luana's Uncle Edison, Aunt Rose, and cousins Harris and Giana, ages four and five.

"My darling niece Luana! How are you, my dear?" Lady Rose asks, curtsying to Luana.

"Aunt Rose, a pleasure to see you again. I'm doing well. How are you?" Luana replies, curtsying to her aunt.

After the greetings and pleasantries, the group sits down to dinner in the dining hall.

The dining hall is long, and has big long windows surrounding the room, except for the wall where the double doors are leading to the hallway. The mahogany dining table is about twenty-four feet long and has brown and gold chairs.

The first course is a peaswallow soup – a cross between a peacock and a swallow. After the appetizer of soup, the main course – roasted quatch – is served with smashed potatoes and garden vegetables. A quatch is a cross between a quail and a nuthatch.

During the main course, Lady Rose turns to her sister, Queen Juniper.

"Have you any luck finding your daughter a proper suitor?"

"No, not yet. She turns away any and all suitors. Luana is only interested in marrying one person: her lady-in-waiting."

"Her lady-in-waiting is not a proper suitor! Besides, spell casters can't marry royals, and vice versa. Besides, how would they even produce an heir?"

"I'm sure they would find some way. But Carter and I won't allow them to be together because of the old traditions."

"I'm surprised you're even allowing *maidens* to court Luana."

"These times are changing, Rose. It's time we moved into the 30th century."

"Well, I won't be moving there any time soon. I won't tell you how to raise your daughter or run this country, but I will tell you this: history has a way of catching up to people. You would do well to make sure that Hartreusia has a set line of heirs for the foreseeable future."

"You make a good point, Rose. I'll think about it."

"That's all I ask."

Soon, dessert is served – chocolate lava cake with starberry sauce and ice cream – and, afterwards, Harris and Giana ask Nona to demonstrate her magic.

"Giana, Harris, hush. Miss Nona has duties to attend to, being Luana's lady-in-waiting."

"It's fine, Your Ladyship. I'd be happy to demonstrate my magic for your children."

"Very well." Rose leaves to chat with her sister once again, and Nona turns to the Morrison siblings.

"I will do the spell only once, so pay attention."

"Yes, Miss Nona."

"First, Harris, I will need an object in your hand."

"Oooh! Oooh! How about a napkin shaped like a peaswallow?"

"That's perfect, Giana."

"What do I have to do?" Harris asks.

"Just stand very still."

Harris begins to stand as still as a sculpture. Nona takes out her small ball of yarn, only measuring an inch or so in diameter, and draws out an inch of yarn. She closes her eyes.

"Sleight of Hand." Nona whispers into her palm.

The peaswallow-shaped napkin shimmers from Harris' hand and disappears, soon reappearing in Nona's outstretched hand.

After cutting the inch of magicless yarn, Nona cuts it in half and she hands one piece of yarn to Harris and the other to Giana.

"Wow." Harris and Giana say in unison.

"They're yours to keep. Take good care of those pieces of yarn."

"Thank you, Miss Nona!"

"You're welcome."

Nona smiles at the two youngsters. When she looks up, she sees Luana's chair is empty, and heads out to try and find her.

Nona locates her in the garden, looking at and smelling the roses.

"I knew I'd find you out here. What are you doing?"

"I can't lie to you, Nona. I had to get away...from the...magic. Seeing your magic for the first time in five years, it brought me right back to the accident."

"Oh, Luana. I'm so sorry. I wasn't thinking."

"It's fine."

"No, it's not. I should've thought of you when I answered your cousins, and I didn't. I'm sorry, Luana."

"I forgive you."

Nona kisses Luana on the cheek.

"Just kiss me, you dork." Luana says, pulling Nona's collar towards her and kissing her on the lips.

The kiss lasts for only a minute, but for Luana and Nona, it feels like an eternity, and the best eternity possible at that.

When the kiss ends, Luana and Nona go back into the castle.

"Luana, dear, whatever were you doing out in the garden at this time of night?" Queen Juniper asks.

"I'm fine, Mother."

"You're avoiding my question."

"I just needed to get away...from...from the magic."

Juniper leads Luana away from all of the hubbub, Nona following closely behind, but not too close as to hear the private conversation of her betters.

"Oh, of course you did. No one blames you for that, dearest. I should have known to get you a new lady-in-waiting as soon as that accident occurred."

"Mother, Nona is fine. It's *me* that's the problem, not her."

"Now, don't go blaming yourself for something she should know better than to do. Which is, Nona?" Juniper asks, looking back at Nona.

"Not using magic unless it's absolutely necessary, Your Highness."

"Correct."

When Juniper, Luana and Nona round the corner, a guard approaches the queen.

"Your Majesty, if I could have a word with you about your security detail for the trip to Indigonia next month."

"Of course. If you'll excuse me, my dear."

"Of course, Mother." Luana says as she and Nona both curtsy to Queen Juniper.

As soon as Queen Juniper and the guard are out of earshot, Luana and Nona head up to the library to read for a while in front of the fireplace.

They each pick up a novel from the romance section and begin to read to each other while sitting on the floor in front of the fireplace.

~.~

"'And with the dust coming from the old books, so, too, do the ashes spread from the urn into the fireplace. Frederick and Liam did not know that they had been followed from the king's funeral pyre, and thus proceeded to lock lips for the foreseeable future, only to be stopped by the king's royal guards. The guards forced the two boys apart and sent them to their rooms. The next morning, both boys were discovered dead. If they could not be together in life, they could always be together in death.'"

"That ending always gets to me, Luana, and it forever makes me think...what if people didn't accept your being gay? Would we share the same fate as Liam and Frederick?" Nona asks.

"I hope not. After all, the king in this story has more than one son, so, if Liam didn't end up being king, then Jeremy would. But, in real life, I'm the only heir to my mother's throne. And if I don't find a suitor in time for my eighteenth birthday...the kingdom would be passed on to Giana." Luana remarks.

"But she's only five."

"Meaning that, if my parents died prematurely, the kingdom would go thirteen years without a ruler."

"And the kingdom would fall to ruin in those years."

"Hey, you don't know that."

"True. Come on, Princess. It's time I help you get ready for bed."

"I'm not even tired." Luana says, yawning.

"That yawn says otherwise. Let's go." Nona rises and helps Luana to her feet, and the two head back to Luana's room to dress for bed.

~ Two ~

Nona wakes up the next morning, and she realizes she's almost out of her magic ball of yarn.

Panicking, she grabs a ruler from her desk and measures the ball of yarn and see it measures about an inch in diameter.

"I better be careful how I use my magic until I go on the quest." Nona tells herself.

She later goes upstairs from the servants' quarters, and heads into Luana's room to awaken her.

Nona has been in this room thousands of times in the past decade or so, but it always amazes her how spacious the bedroom is of the crown princess of Hartreusia.

When Nona opens the double doors to Luana's room, and as she walks in, she sees the cream vanity with a gold and cream chair. Near the vanity is the windowseat with a window above it. The windowseat has cream pillows and a cream-cushioned seat. Everything in this room has cream and gold tones and undertones. The four-poster bed, next to the first window, has a canopy above it. The wood on the four-poster bed has been painted gold, and the comforter, pillows, and blankets are all cream. The walls are a cream-and-gold floral wallpaper.

On the other side of the bed is another windowseat with a window, the same look as the other. Next to that window, up against the wall, is the brown-and-gold changing screen, with floral decorations all throughout. Across the room from the bed is the bathroom, and in the bathroom, there is a toilet next to the sink, a sink against the wall facing the door and a bathtub to the left of the doorway up against the one window in the bathroom. The cream bathtub, cream sink and cream toilet all have gold fixtures.

"Princess? It's time to wake up." Nona says, approaching the sleeping - and snoring - princess.

Luana opens one eye, and smiles at her girlfriend.

"Time to wake up, Princess, and greet the day."

"I'm up. I'm up."

Luana sits up and stretches.

"So, Luana, what's on the agenda for today?"

"Well, Mother and Father have arranged suitors to come and meet me so I may choose one as my future spouse."

"All before breakfast?"

"No, silly. But just after."

"Do you think I'll be able to attend the meeting with you?"

"I doubt it, Nona, since both Mother and Father know we're so close."

"I see. Well, let me help you look presentable for your suitors."

Nona helps Luana get ready for the day, dressing her in a simple blue and silver gown and silver tiara, perfect for both eating and courting.

When the girls go down for breakfast, Queen Juniper performs her inspection on her daughter.

"Very nice, Luana. Very nice indeed. I'm sure both men and maidens would be pleased to see you in this gown."

"Thank you, Mother."

"You're welcome. Now, eat your breakfast. Nona, I assume you'll be keeping yourself busy during the interview portions of the courting?"

"Yes, Your Majesty."

"Good. I wouldn't want anyone thinking that Luana favors you over any royal suitors."

After everyone eats their breakfast, Nona heads down to the servants' quarters to start her chores, while Luana, her mother, and father head to the throne room, so the suitors can begin their interviews.

Soon, Luana stands between her parents' thrones, her mother sitting to her left, and her father sitting to her right.

"Send in the first suitor." King Carter says.

A girl with dark skin, black hair and green eyes comes in, wearing a gold dress and a silver tiara.

"Presenting, Her Ladyship, Lady Rosemary of Castle Cantrell in Indigonia."

"Your Highnesses, I am delighted to make your acquaintance."

"Likewise, Your Ladyship. Princess Luana, you may begin." Queen Juniper says.

Luana steps down from the platform and begins circling Lady Rosemary.

"Indigonia is farthest in terms of alliance to Hartreusia. Is that correct, Lady Rosemary?"

"Yes, Your Highness."

"And what do you hope to gain from marrying into the Atteberry family?"

"Love and respect, Your Highness."

"Are you saying your family does not provide you with such, Lady Rosemary?"

"No, Your Highness. I meant to say *additional* love and respect. I misspoke."

"Very well. Lady Rosemary, what do you like to do for fun?"

"Well, Your Highness, I like to ride my horse, read, write, and practice my violin."

"Are you a trained violinist?"

"Yes, Your Highness. I've been playing the violin since I was five years old."

"Do you bake?"

"No, Your Highness, but my girlfriend – I mean, my *best* friend – does."

Luana struggles to keep her cool.

"Lady Rosemary, you mean to tell me that you are already *with* someone?" Luana asks, smiling through gritted teeth.

"Yes, Your Highness."

"You are dismissed, Your Ladyship."

After Lady Rosemary curtsies and leaves the room, Luana goes back up to stand between her parents.

"Presenting, Her Ladyship, Lady Isabella of Castle Villareal in Rosiary."

Lady Isabella comes in, her black hair in an intricate braid and wearing a red dress.

"Your Majesties, I come offering myself as Princess Luana's suitor and future spouse."

"And what do you have to offer, Lady Isabella, besides yourself?" Queen Juniper asks.

"I can offer cooking and baking skills that rival anyone else's, along with being extremely good at archery and writing, if I do say so myself, so any royal correspondence can be done by myself." Lady Isabella starts laughing, and she accidentally snorts.

"Oh, pardon me, Your Majesties."

"It's quite alright, Your Ladyship." Luana says.

"Thank you for your consideration, Your Highnesses." Lady Isabella says, curtsying. She then leaves, and Luana once again steps back up to the platform between her parents.

Once Lady Isabella leaves, a young man takes her place.

"Presenting, His Lordship, Lord Arthur of Castle Arellano in Lavenderia."

Luana steps forward to greet this young man.

"Lord Arthur," Luana says, curtsying.

"Princess Luana. It's quite a pleasure to make your acquaintance," Lord Arthur says, bowing and kissing Luana's outstretched hand.

"The pleasure is all mine, Your Lordship. So, what makes you think you're worthy to become king of Hartreusia, and of Gnypso?"

"Your Highness, I can bring you all the jewels and wealth you could ever want. Exotic foods from distant lands, exotic furs and perfumes."

"You believe you can buy my love?"

"Of course. For what more could you want than me as your king and life partner?"

"Thank you for your offer. We'll be in touch should we need you further."

"Thank you, Your Highness. It was a pleasure to meet all of you, and I hope that one day, we can be man and wife."

Lord Arthur leaves and Luana heads back to stand between her parents' thrones. She struggles to not roll her eyes at Lord Arthur's behavior.

"Stay calm, Luana. This will all be over before you know it, and, hopefully, we'll have a lord or lady to rule by your side when the time comes. Remember, Luana, your mother and I only want the best for you."

"And the best would be to marry me off to someone I could never truly love?"

"Luana!"

"Juniper, it's fine. She will learn in due time that love takes a lot of time and work, and it doesn't form overnight."

"Father, that's what I'm trying to tell you. I could never love someone that doesn't know me."

"That's why there will be a period of courtship for the person you choose to get to know you and for you to get to know them."

"I understand, Father."

The next few suitors come in, and, after presenting themselves, they leave.

Knowing she can't marry Nona, only one person has peaked Luana's interest.

"So, Luana, have you made your decision on who will court you for the next few months?"

"Yes, Father. I choose...Lady Isabella."

"An excellent choice. Lady Isabella of Castle Villareal in Rosiary. Ciara?"

"Yes, Your Majesty?" The royal page asks, appearing at the king's side.

"Please send Lady Isabella back in. Princess Luana has made her decision."

"Right away, Your Majesty."

Soon, Lady Isabella comes back in.

"You wanted to see me, Your Majesties?"

"Yes, Lady Isabella. Princess Luana has made her decision." King Carter prompts his daughter forward to voice her decision.

"I choose you, Lady Isabella, for courtship."

"I am delighted to get to know you better, Princess Luana, and I look forward to seeing you more in the coming months leading up to the royal wedding."

"I'm elated to get to know you better as well, Lady Isabella."

Within the next week, Lady Isabella moves from Rosiary with her family into one of the spare rooms in the castle in Hartreusia with her belongings and is given time to get used to being around the royal family.

Meanwhile, Nona has been getting ready to go on the quest. There's just one thing missing: her companion.

She finds Luana and Isabella in the library, reading to each other from romance novels.

"Princess Luana, Lady Isabella. I didn't expect to find you here."

"King Carter and Queen Juniper want me to spend as much time as possible with Princess Luana, so we may get acquainted."

"I see. Princess Luana, may I speak with you for a moment?"

"Of course, Nona. I'll be right back, m'lady."

"Take as much time as you need, Princess. I'm not going anywhere."

Luana and Nona go to a secluded part of the library.

"Luana, what are you doing? I thought you wanted to marry *me*!"

"I did – do. But my parents wouldn't let up about the courtship, so I had to choose someone that was a royal."

"So you chose the girl from my home country."

"You'll learn to love her, Nona. As will I."

"I don't like this, Luana, and neither should you."

"What's *that* supposed to mean?"

"I just mean that you shouldn't get too comfortable around Lady Isabella."

"And why is that?"

"Because...she just doesn't sit right with me."

"You're just jealous, Nona. Not everyone is out to get me, you know. Now, if you'll excuse me, I have a courtship to get back to."

"This isn't over, Luana!"

But Luana is already gone.

Nona gets her things together for the quest: sensible shoes, sun hats, sleeping bag, a pocket knife, water carrier, compass, a map, cloaks, and food.

All that's left is to see where she's going to go.

Soon, Nona heads back to the library to talk with Justine, the librarian.

"Hey, Justine. I was wondering...you went on the quest, right?"

"I sure did. What's this all about, Nona?"

"Well, I'm about to go on the quest myself, and I was wondering if you knew where to go."

"I'm afraid I don't. No one knows where the girl is who spins the magic yarn. But what I can tell you is there's a tavern in Lavenderia called The Keen Couple. Maybe the owners could help you along the way. Now, Nona, have you chosen your companion?"

"I...I have, but I don't think they'll be able to go. They might be too busy."

"All you have to do is ask them, Nona. Surely, they're not too busy for you."

"I'll have to see. Thanks for the advice, Justine."

"You're welcome."

Nona soon leaves the library to continue preparing for the quest.

In the evening, Luana, Nona, and Isabella have gone their separate ways for the night: Nona to her room in the servants' quarters, Isabella to her guest suite, and Luana to her bedchamber.

Luana sits at her window overlooking the ocean and the lighthouse, and she begins to sing a siren's song.

Ooooh, ooooh
Ooooh, ooooh
As the tide turns into mist
As the sea turns into air
Will each sailor fall into despair
Or will they fall in love with care
As the siren sings
Inside your dreams
Will they be alone but fair?
As no affair is right
As the birds fly in the night
Will each sailor end in plight?
Or will they be filled with delight?
Ooooh, ooooh
Ooooh, ooooh

Off in the distance, Luana can see the lighthouse and the ships coming into shore.

~.~

Lady Isabella is reading from a romance novel on her windowseat when she hears a voice calling to her from what she thinks is beyond the castle grounds.

She becomes enchanted by the voice, and, unbeknownst to her, becomes enchanted by Luana.

~ Three ~

The following morning, Luana awakens to a knock at her door.

"I'm coming!" She announces.

Luana pulls back the covers and sleepily gets out of bed and goes to her door, opening it to reveal –

"Lady Isabella? Are you alright?"

"Yes, Your Highness. It's strange. I must've had a dream last night that I was being enchanted."

"Enchanted?"

"I think by a siren. That's what it sounded like anyway."

"Did you have your windows open, by any chance?"

"That's another strange thing: my windows were closed and locked. How could I have heard the siren's song from *inside* the castle?"

"That is quite a strange occurrence. Why don't you head on downstairs to breakfast, and I'll meet you there in a few minutes?"

"Of course, Your Highness." Lady Isabella curtsies and heads down the hall to go downstairs to meet the king, queen, and her parents, Lord Dustin and Lady Alissa, for breakfast.

Soon, Isla helps Luana get dressed for the day, and Luana heads down to breakfast herself.

An uneventful week later, Luana and Isabella head out to one of the garden's many gazebos and sit down.

"Princess Luana?"

"Yes, Lady Isabella?"

"I was wondering...well, I was actually *hoping* that we could take our relationship to the next level."

"Oh?"

"You see, Your Highness, I've...I've been wanting to ask you something, and I didn't know how to approach you with this question."

"You have nothing to be afraid of, Lady Isabella. You can always ask me anything."

"Alright. Here I go."

Isabella stands up and kneels before Luana.

"Princess Luana, I've only known you for a short time, but I feel a strong connection to you, like a sailor to the sea. I was wondering and hoping, will you be mine for all of eternity? Princess Luana, will you marry me?"

Knowing *she* was the one who enchanted Isabella last week, Luana hesitates in answering. Was this a genuine proposal, or was it because of the enchantment Luana herself had put on Isabella? For some reason, only those without magic, and those that aren't family are able to be enchanted by Luana's songs, but Luana forgets this sometimes.

Still, Luana delays to answer Isabella's life-altering question.

Luana can sense a crowd forming in the castle, and in the garden itself, and that puts more pressure on Luana's answer.

After stalling for a little more than a minute, Luana gets up and faces Isabella.

"Lady Isabella, after much reflection on what we share together, as royals and as a couple, I have decided to accept your request. Yes, Lady Isabella, I will marry you."

"Princess Luana, may I kiss you?"

"Yes, Lady Isabella, you may."

Lady Isabella and Princess Luana seal their engagement with a kiss.

Nona is watching from the windows with the rest of the castle staff, and she is far from happy.

~.~

Luana and Isabella meet with the king and queen to plan the royal engagement ball, and, after that planning meeting, Luana meets Nona in the library, so they can chat about Nona's quest. Or, at least, that's what Nona told Ciara to tell Luana.

"Princess Luana, first and foremost, I'd like to congratulate you on your engagement to Lady Isabella. Nona is waiting for you in the romance section." Justine, the librarian, affirmed.

"Thank you, Justine. I'll head over there now."

Luana heads over to the romance section and finds Nona among the shelves of books.

"Nona, you wanted to see me about your quest?" Luana asks.

"Actually, Princess Luana, I wanted to see you about another matter entirely."

"What is it, Nona?"

"I don't trust Lady Isabella."

"This *again*, Nona? You can't keep complaining about the inevitable. Lady Isabella and I will be getting married, and there's nothing you can do about it."

"Says *you*, maybe."

"I am your future queen, Nona. Once I am queen, I will prove to you that Lady Isabella and I are meant to be together."

"Are you sure about that, Luana? You have barely even known her for a week and already you're engaged. Don't you think you're taking this thing a little too fast?"

"No, I don't. It's true love."

"What do you know about true love, Luana? You promised that you'd marry *me*!"

"That was before the courtship started!"

"Which has barely had a week to form. I don't think you should carelessly agree to marry someone you barely even know."

"That's one person's opinion, Nona. And, last time I checked, if I wanted your opinion on the subject, I would have asked for it! Now, if you'll excuse me, Lady Isabella and I need to discuss what we're going to wear to our engagement ball."

"You can't walk away from every problem you face, Luana. You'll never learn that way."

Nona grabs Luana's arm and Luana grabs Nona by her face, and begins to softly sing to her, so no one else will hear.

After the song is over, Nona appears to be in a trance.

"You will leave me alone about your lack of approval of my bride-to-be, Nona. We shall never speak of it again."

Her skirts rustling behind her, Luana heads out of the library, not noticing the indignant look on Nona's face.

The song didn't work on her.

~.~

Nona has a plan to break up Luana and Isabella indefinitely.

And it will all begin at five past nine sharp on Saturday night, at the engagement ball.

But, for now, Nona must resume preparing for her quest.

After getting the supplies necessary for the quest, Nona heads back to her room to secretly prepare her surprise for Princess Luana and Lady Isabella's engagement ball.

That night, Nona hears a familiar voice singing above her.

She now knows that Luana is the "siren" everyone has been hearing, and she decides that, in addition to her surprise, that she will publicly confront Luana about her singing, and that Isabella seems to be under a trance because of Luana's singing.

Nona goes to sleep peacefully that night, knowing that she will be able to exact her revenge on Luana for leaving her and for accepting a proposal too fast for Nona's liking.

~.~

The day after, Nona does her chores as she always does, and heads to the castle's science lab to come up with a concoction to ruin the engagement ball.

Nona knows that she can't poison the food; she'd be hanged for that.

But a simple, harmless little smoke bomb would do just the trick. No one would get hurt, and Luana would be humiliated at her special ball.

After Nona comes up with the formula to create a smoke bomb big enough to fill the entire ballroom, she puts the smoke bomb carefully in her satchel and heads up to help Luana dress for her first public appearance as an engaged princess with Isabella.

"Where have you been, Nona? We were supposed to help the princess dress for her public appearance ten minutes ago." Isla scolds. Isla is another one of Luana's maids.

"I know, Isla. But I'm here now, and that's all that matters."

Isla and Nona head into the princess' bedchamber and help her get ready in a mint green and white gown with bows and off the shoulder three-quarter inch sleeves. Nona places a golden tiara on Luana's braided bun while Isla places black shoes on Luana's feet.

Luana meets her future bride in the hallway in front of the double doors that lead out to the balcony.

Isabella is wearing a light gold gown to go with Luana's mint green ensemble and is wearing a gold tiara on her curled black hair and gold shoes.

After they are announced, Princess Luana and Lady Isabella head out, hand in hand, to the balcony to an expecting crowd, excited to see their future queen and queen consort together at last. The couple is met with cheers and thrown flowers, and the princess and lady are each given a bouquet of irises to say congratulations on their engagement.

Inside, Nona's plan is soon to come to fruition.

~.~

The night of the engagement ball has arrived, and Luana is getting dressed by all of her maids – except for Nona, who is still plotting – in a deep red ball gown to symbolize the passion and love she not only has for her fiancée, but also for her kingdom.

Meanwhile, Isabella is being helped to get dressed in a gown that resembles the night sky – a dark blue gown with silver sequins all throughout.

When Luana and Isabella are finished getting dressed, they head out to meet the king and queen, so that King Carter and Queen Juniper can be announced before the engaged royal couple.

Soon, the merriment and feast are underway, and Nona waits in the shadows for the perfect moment to execute her plan.

While everyone is turned to see Luana and Isabella have their first dance as an engaged couple at exactly 9:05PM, Nona throws out the smoke bomb she had produced, and it explodes like a firework in the night sky.

Screams and shouts erupt from the crowd, and Nona, in her simple purple gown and heels, does her best to look innocent and as bewildered as the rest of the crowd, and that isn't hard, having followed and been under the royals for so many years.

When people turn to try and find the culprit, Nona does the same.

King Carter steps forward and clears his throat.

"I demand to know who threw that smoke bomb. If you come forward, I'll make sure that the punishment for your crime is less than severe."

"Your Majesty, these were found in the servants' quarters. We believe that one of the servants is conspiring against the engagement of Princess Luana and Lady Isabella." Ciara says, coming up to the king and queen and curtsying while holding up Nona's satchel with the ingredients for a smoke bomb.

"Thank you, Ciara."

"You're welcome, Your Majesty."

Ciara steps away, and the king and queen look over the crowd, trying to see if they can spot the perpetrator.

"Until further notice, and until the felon is caught, not one servant is allowed outside of the castle grounds. But come forward, and only the criminal will be prosecuted." King Carter tells the concerned crowd.

"That will be all the festivities for now. Please leave and stay in your homes. We apologize that we have to cut the party short, but we fear there may be further attacks. Thank you and good night." Queen Juniper advises.

After the party guests leave, Luana and Isabella approach King Carter and Queen Juniper.

"Your Majesties, if I may, if I hadn't quickly proposed to Princess Luana after barely a week of knowing her – " Isabella starts.

"Lady Isabella, I hope you're not blaming yourself for something someone else did, because you shouldn't. Whoever did this is someone that does not want to see you and

Princess Luana happy. Do not worry about this, as King Carter and I will make sure the person who did this is rightfully imprisoned." Queen Juniper observes.

"Thank you, Your Majesties."

"You're quite welcome. I would advise that you and Princess Luana stay in the same bedchamber for the time being. We will have guards posted outside your room to make sure no one is able to get in and cause further harm. You are both dismissed."

After curtsying to the king and queen, Luana and Isabella head up to Luana's bedchambers to get ready for bed.

After Luana gets dressed in her bathroom while Isabella gets dressed behind the changing screen, the two meet at either side of Luana's queen-sized bed.

"After you, Your Highness."

"No, no, Your Ladyship, after *you*."

"If you insist, Princess."

"I do, m'lady."

After the two get into bed and head off to sleep, Queen Juniper quietly opens the door to see the two girls sound asleep, and smiles softly to herself.

Whoever could have sabotaged the girls' engagement party?

~.~

King Carter paces in front of his throne, and Queen Juniper is sitting on her throne, wondering what she can do to ease her husband's troubled mind.

"Carter, why don't you head to bed, and I'll foresee the criminal's conviction and punishment."

"Juniper, I can't sleep while someone within the castle is conspiring against our little girl and her fiancée. This just isn't right."

"Do we know for sure it was someone in the castle, and not someone in the village?"

"Are you saying Ciara was lying?"

"Not lying, Carter, but misled."

"You saw the crowd's response to the engagement. If there was at least one person that didn't agree with it, they didn't show it."

"We can't protect our daughter from everything, Carter, even if we are the king and queen."

"We can certainly try, Juniper."

"While that may be true, we should try to rest. Anyone who could conspire against Luana or the crown would have a hard time doing it tonight, with guards posted outside every door."

"That wouldn't stop them from trying."

"We'll have to get some guards to post outside the windows of the castle, just to be safe."

"I agree. Ciara?"

"Yes, Your Majesty?"

"Get some guards to make their posts outside every first-floor window of the castle."

"At once, Your Majesty." Ciara curtsies to her king and queen and heads out to see the head of the royal guard.

The king and queen soon head up to bed themselves, and wonder who could have done such a thing. But that question would have to wait until tomorrow, when everyone is rested.

Carter sits up in bed.

"Dear? What is it?" Juniper asks.

"What if someone is conspiring against the crown and plans to sneak out in the middle of the night to escape and get more followers?"

"The guards will make sure that doesn't happen. Now, please, dear, try to get some sleep."

"I will, Juniper. Good night, my queen."

"Good night, my king."

~.~

Down in the servants' quarters, Nona is planning on escaping to head to Rosiary, where her extended family is.

"Nona, what are you doing? It's the middle of the night." Isla asks.

"I just...need to get some air."

"With the guards posted outside every door? There's no way you could get out. Why are you trying to leave in the middle of the night?" Isla suddenly gasps.

"Are *you* the one who set off that smoke bomb last night? Nona! You *have* to turn yourself in."

"I don't *have* to do anything, Isla."

"Uh, yeah, you do. If the guards catch you, the king and queen would probably have your head for committing such a crime."

"They wouldn't do anything to me. They know how close Princess Luana and I are to each other, and they can't risk anything happening to me. Which is why – "

"You committed the perfect crime. To stop the marriage from happening. Nona, how selfish can you get? Jeopardizing all of those people for your own personal needs? Try thinking of others once in a while!"

"I've been thinking of others for the past thirteen years, since Princess Luana and I became friends. Isla, I can't have this argument with you right now. I have to leave."

"And abandon your best friend of thirteen years?"

"She's got Lady Isabella. They've got a whole lifetime to spend together, so why should I care what she thinks?"

"I know why you did this: you're jealous of Lady Isabella's affections for Princess Luana."

"That's preposterous. That's absurd. That's ridiculous. That's – "

"The reason you sabotaged the ball? Nona, you need to stop thinking about yourself so much."

"I haven't had time to think about myself for –"

"The past thirteen years. I *know*. But, obviously, you only thought about yourself last night. So either go turn yourself in to the king and queen, or I will."

"Isla, is that a threat?"

"No. It's a promise. I can't have you sabotaging the rest of us for your own selfish interests."

Isla leaves the room, and, mysteriously, goes out to get a guard to turn Nona in.

About four minutes later, when Nona has just about finished packing, someone knocks on the door to Nona and Isla's bedroom.

"Nona Hamlett?"

It's one of the guards.

"Nona, we know you're in there. If you come forward, I'm sure King Carter will give you a punishment that is less than severe."

"How do I know I can trust you? You're a guard! You're above me in rank."

"Above rank or not, we *both* serve the crown, and we can't have anyone conspiring against it."

Nona secretly pulls out her dagger and, putting it behind her back, opens the door.

"If you think I'm going to come quietly, I have other ideas." Nona says, brandishing her dagger and pointing it at the guard. The guard puts his hands up.

"Nona, I can help you. But only if you turn yourself in. You can't run away from this."

"I can if you let me go."

"And be punished for treason? I don't think so."

"Punished for this, punished for that...can't we all just get along?"

"We *were* getting along until that little stunt of yours at the ball last night. If you come with us, you can meet with the king and queen in the morning. You'll have to stay in the dungeon for the time being."

"The *dungeon*? You're acting as if I committed a horrible crime, and not just a little party trick."

"You put the party guests *and* the royal family at risk for danger. Nona, come on."

The guard harshly grabs Nona's arm and escorts her down to the dungeon and locks her in a cell.

"I'll come get you in the morning, so you can have an audience with Their Majesties."

~.~

Nona doesn't sleep that night, not knowing what else to do but pace around in her cell.

All she had done was a simple party trick, nothing more; she hadn't intended to harm anyone. And no one *was* harmed.

~.~

The next morning, the guard takes Nona out of her cell and cuffs her hands in shackles.

"What am I, a common criminal? I'm the princess' best friend."

"We'll see what the princess has to say for your behavior last night. Move it."

The guard leads Nona up to the throne room where King Carter, Princess Luana and Queen Juniper are waiting for her, a cross look on all of their faces. King Carter is wearing his royal robe and crown, while Queen Juniper is wearing an orange gown and her crown. Princess Luana is wearing the same gown she wore to the ball last night.

"Nona? *You* were the one who set off the smoke bomb last night?"

"Luana, stand down. Let me do the talking."

"Yes, Father."

"Nona, would you care to explain yourself?" King Carter asks.

"Yes, Your Majesty."

"Go on."

"Well, you see, Your Majesties, it just so happens that...Princess Luana is a siren, and she tried to get me to stop being jealous of her and Lady Isabella."

"We are well aware of our daughter's siren powers. Her grandmother was part siren as well."

"But she tried to enchant me to stop being jealous of her and Lady Isabella!"

"Nona, you used a smoke bomb at the party last night. That's a major infraction compared to Princess Luana's siren song."

"So, you're not going to punish her, Your Majesty?"

"Why would I punish my daughter for something she is doing to calm herself?"

"Calm herself? She's luring sailors to their deaths, and I'm sure she enchanted Lady Isabella as well."

"That is enough, Nona. Now, I would hang you for treason, but seeing as my daughter would be miserable without you, Queen Juniper and I have decided, instead, to send the three of you girls on the quest to get you to work together. No guards, just each other and your horses and what you can carry on your backs."

"But Your Majesty!"

"No buts. Unless you'd prefer me to send you back to the dungeon for the rest of your life."

"No, Your Majesty. I will accept your offer."

"Good. You have a week for this quest, and, after a week, regardless of whether or not you have found the girl who spins the magic yarn, you will return home. If the three of you have not worked out your differences, I'm afraid that you, Nona, will be sent away to the Convent of the Seven Deities."

~ Four ~

Nona couldn't believe her ears. If the quest failed, no, if *she* failed to get along with Luana and Isabella, she'd be sent away to the Convent of the Seven Deities.

"The Convent?!" Nona is shocked.

"Yes. Before you leave, Queen Juniper and I will pray over the three of you, so that the gods and goddesses will watch over you and be with you on your quest. Go get ready to leave."

"Wait, we're leaving *now*?" Nona questions.

"As soon as you have gathered all of the supplies necessary, you must leave. Princess Luana, go get yourself and Lady Isabella prepared for the quest." Queen Juniper instructs.

"Yes, Mother."

After Luana leaves, Nona turns to leave herself, but King Carter stops her.

"Nona, there is one more thing Queen Juniper and I must tell you: do not let any harm come to Princess Luana or Lady Isabella or yourself during this quest."

"Do I even get a choice here, Your Majesty? Don't I get to think this over?"

"Very well. I will give you five minutes to think about this offer, then I will need your answer."

Nona turns away from the king and queen, and she out-weighs her options: going on the quest with her seemingly ex-girlfriend and her ex-girlfriend's fiancée, or spend some time in the dungeon alone and ultimately not be able to use magic.

Right now, the dungeon doesn't seem like too bad of an option. But, nevertheless, Nona must do what's right for the kingdom, and not for herself, and that would be to go on the quest with Princess Luana and Lady Isabella.

The five minutes are up faster than Nona expects, and King Carter clears his throat to get her attention.

"Well, Nona? Have you made your decision?"

"I have, Your Majesty, and I have decided that I will do everything in my power to protect Princess Luana, Lady Isabella and myself."

"A wise decision. You are dismissed."

Soon, Nona has gathered all of the supplies needed for the quest, and she meets King Carter, Queen Juniper, Princess Luana, Lady Isabella and Isabella's parents at the back stables.

All around them, people kneel on their left knee, close their eyes and place their hands behind their backs, and wait for King Carter to start the prayer to the gods and goddesses of Destiny. The royals and Nona kneel, close their eyes and place their hands behind their backs as well.

"Oh, Aileen, goddess of all humans and creatures; Nellie, goddess of healing; Erik, god of magic; Irah, god of nature; Loana, goddess of wisdom; Era, goddess of time; and Sena, goddess of beauty; I pray to you yesterday, today, tomorrow and forever to watch over and be with Nona Hamlett of Rosiary, Princess Luana Atteberry of Hartreusia, and Lady Isabella Villareal of Rosiary, to heal them if they get hurt, to guide Nona as she uses her magic, to help them get through the forests of uncertainty, to help them make wise decisions, to help them manage their time, and to help them be beautiful in any and all ways. By the power of the seven deities, so be it."

"So be it." The voices echo around the king.

The people rise from their kneeling and go about their business.

"Be safe, be true, be the best people you are meant to be." Queen Juniper says as Princess Luana, Lady Isabella and Nona mount their assigned horses.

Luana will be taking a different horse from her own, so as not to cause suspicion, and she and Isabella will both be wearing cloaks so they won't be recognized.

The girls head out beyond the castle grounds, beyond the gate, to the bridge between Hartreusia and Lavenderia.

"We don't know if sirens are going to be a problem, so we must be on our guard." Nona warns, looking at Luana.

"What are you looking at me for? Yes, I'm part siren, but that doesn't mean I'm on their side!"

"Just checking, Luana. By the way, you and Isabella will be going under pseudonyms for the duration of the trip, and you will let me do the talking, just in case anyone should recognize your voices. Is that understood?"

"Yes, *Your Highness*." Luana quips. Nona ignores the snide comment.

"Luana, you will be known as Louisa, and Isabella, you will be known as Isla."

"Will we go anywhere for meals, or will we be fending for ourselves?" Isabella asks.

"I've packed us meals for the next week, but we can stop for a treat on the way to our destination, as well as for directions. Justine said something about a tavern called The Keen Couple, and the owners might know where the girl is who spins the magic yarn."

The girls travel for about an hour and come upon the tavern, The Keen Couple. There's a sign posted outside that says "No Magic Allowed Within These Walls".

"By the seven deities, what if we get into trouble, Nona? What then?" Luana asks.

"We use our skills instead of my magic. Isla, do you have any fighting skills?"

"I have archery skills. I brought my bow and arrow from home."

"Good. We might need it. But, if a fight breaks out, you let me handle it, alright?"

"I am quite capable of handling myself in a fight."

"While that may be true, you're an important asset in Louisa's life, so there will be no fighting on your part. And you're both servant girls like me who work for Princess Luana."

"Then why did you ask if I had any fighting skills, if you won't let me use them?"

"It's just in case we need you to fight. Understood?"

"Understood, Nona."

"Very well. Let's go in."

The three girls dismount their horses and head into the tavern.

The exterior of the tavern has a sign with the name of the tavern, and has a post to tie up their horses. The tavern has a mahogany bar with brown cushioned barstools, and it has brown walls. Behind the bar are shelves full of mead, beer, and other alcoholic beverages. There are tables around the tavern, with chairs and stools, depending on the height of the table. Everything about this tavern is brown, except for some of the patrons and the five workers. The tavern is currently buzzing with lively patrons, and the smell of beer, mead, and other alcoholic drinks wafts through the air, and there is a slight fragrance of roasting meat.

Luana, Isabella and Nona sit at one of the tables in between the bar and the exit, just in case there is a need to make a hasty escape after ordering a treat.

There's a tough-looking woman at the counter with light brown hair, fair skin and green eyes.

"Welcome to The Keen Couple! My wife, Julia, will be with you in just a moment." The woman at the counter cheerfully crows.

"Thank you." Nona says. She leans her head in at the table they're sitting at, and Luana and Isabella do the same.

"Make sure to keep your cloaks up, and remember to let *me* do the talking."

Luana and Isabella nod at Nona, and sit back just as Julia approaches the table with three menus filled with the day's drink and food choices.

"If you ladies would take a glance at the menu, I'll be back to take your orders."

"Thank you."

Soon after, Julia comes back to take the girls' orders.

"What'll it be, ladies?"

"We'll have the chocolate lava cake with starberry sauce and ice cream, please." Nona says.

"Three spoons?"

"That'll do. Thank you."

"You're welcome. I'll be back soon with your order."

Nona looks around at her surroundings, and sees the patrons going about their business in the tavern. Some are eating and chatting with their friends, while others are sipping their drinks and reading the daily paper, *Lavenderia News.*

Julia returns about five minutes later with the girls' order, and she places it down with the three spoons and some napkins.

"Thank you, Julia. Question: do you and your wife know anything about where the girl is who spins the magic yarn?"

"Ah, we have a spell caster in our midst, Holly. On the quest, are you?"

"Yes."

"Well, the most we can tell you is that she wipes the memory of anyone who meets her so they won't remember who or where she is."

"How do you know that if she wipes memories?"

"It's only a rumor. But a steady rumor at that. Enjoy your treat, ladies, and let me know if I can get you anything else."

"Thank you, Julia."

"You're welcome."

The girls dig in to their chocolate lava cake and the cake has a rich chocolatey taste, while the starberry sauce is sour yet sweet, and the ice cream is creamy and familiar. They polish it off quite quickly, and Julia soon comes by with the check.

Nona quickly pays her the ten zikapia, so she, Luana and Isabella can leave and continue on their journey.

"Ladies, fair warning: there are many dangers here in Lavenderia." Holly says.

"But you won't tell us what they are, will you?" Nona asks.

"We would if we could, but there's a law regarding the quest that says we can tell you there *are* dangers, but we can't tell you *what* those dangers are, or even *where* they are. We're sorry. Good luck on the rest of the quest, ladies. We'll be rooting for you." Julia says.

"Thank you for the advice, and your hospitality. It means a lot to us."

The girls get up and head towards the door, but, before Nona can put her hand on the handle, the door swings open, revealing a band of five thieves, led by a woman.

"Put your hands up, and no one gets hurt." The woman says, drawing her sword.

Nona puts Luana and Isabella behind her and backs up, drawing her own sword. She turns to Holly and Julia, who have their swords drawn.

"Protect my girlfriends Louisa and Isla. They mean the world to me."

"Will do." Holly says. Holly, Julia and Nona back up to the back wall and protect Luana and Isabella at all sides as the leader of the thieves approaches them.

Nona lunges and the leader of the thieves parries, blocking Nona's move, and prepares a counter attack by riposte.

The match continues, and, soon, the leader of the band of thieves surrenders to Nona.

"I yield. You're quite the worthy opponent."

"Thank you. Now leave while you still have your lives."

"You sure you don't wanna join us?"

"I'm sure. I've got better things to do."

"Suit yourself. If you ever need someone to fight off something for you when you're outnumbered, give me a call." The leader says, handing her holographic business card to Nona.

"Matilde Northrup: Thief and Leader of the Band of Dangerous Deviants."

"That's our name. Again, if you need a band of deviants to help, give us a call at that number."

"Thank you." The Dangerous Deviants leave the tavern, and there's a sigh of relief. Nona plugs the name and number on the card into her smart phone.

"You really handled yourself there, girlie. What's your name?" Julia asks.

"I'm Nona, and, once again, the girls you helped protect are Louisa and Isla. We work at Castle Atteberry in Hartreusia for Princess Luana."

"I see. So you must know all the princess' secrets, do you?"

Nona steps back, appalled. Holly bursts out laughing.

"I'm just kidding. Secrets are secrets, and they should stay that way. We'll let you get back to your quest. Good luck, ladies, and take care. If you're ever back at The Keen Couple, we'd be happy to serve you again."

"Thank you, Holly and Julia."

"You're welcome."

The girls head out of the tavern and mount their horses and head on their way to the girl who spins the magic yarn.

They don't notice a young man spying on them and following them from a distance.

The girls stop at a stream to refill their canteens and give the horses a drink, and the young man is watching them from a group of bushes.

"They're just...talking..." The young man whispers into his phone.

"Can you make out any of it?" A woman whispers back to him.

"They're just talking about where they're going to head next, and they're trying to guess what the first challenge will be."

"Did they see you among the Dangerous Deviants?"

"If they did, they didn't pay close attention to me."

"Good. The last thing we need is for you to be recognized and have my plan ruined."

"Don't worry about it. If they spot me, I'll just play the injured beggar card."

"Good call, Emmitt. I'll see you soon."

Emmitt hangs up his phone and continues to spy on the girls.

~ Five ~

The girls continue on their quest, and, before they reach the first challenge, Nona brings up something to Luana, but using her and Isabella's code names so their cover won't be blown in case anyone is following them or overhearing them.

"I have a question for you, Louisa."

"What is it, Nona?"

"Why did you say yes to Isla's proposal? You barely knew each other for a week before she proposed."

"I know that, Nona. But I'm willing to have a lifetime to get to know her better."

"Louisa, that's not a very good plan. You have to know someone before they propose or you propose. And you have to make sure they're the real deal, and not just some phony."

"You're just jealous of what Isla and I have, Nona."

"Why would I be jealous? You're both nonspellers while I'm a spell caster."

"Yes, but you're limited by what you can do with your power. And nonspellers have more power than you know." Luana gallops far ahead of Nona and Isabella, who can only follow after her.

"Louisa! Stop!"

"Whoa, girl. WHOA!" Luana shouts to her horse.

Luana stops before a field of thorns. They're red and big and the girls don't see an end in sight.

"Louisa!"

Luana looks behind her and sees Nona and Isabella galloping toward her.

"Are you alright?"

"I'm okay. Isla, if you hadn't called out, I would've been done for. Thank you."

"You're welcome. Nona, how are we going to get across this field of thorns?"

"With magic. Once I say this spell, I need you to both take one of my hands, and not let go until we're past the field of thorns. We need to work as a team. Are we ready?"

Isabella and Luana look at each other, then back at Nona, and nod.

"Ready."

"Okay." Nona takes out her magic ball of yarn and places it in between the saddle and the horse so it won't fall.

"Abracadabra." An inch of yarn shimmers and fades to a pale purple. Instantly, Luana and Isabella grab each of Nona's hands and they begin to guide the horses slowly through the field of thorns.

"Whatever you do, don't speed up and don't let go of me."

"What does this spell do exactly?" Isabella asks.

"It makes the spell caster and anyone who touches them impervious to anything."

"I like this spell."

"I do, too. Hang tight, girls. I can see the end of the field in sight."

The girls eventually reach the end of the field of thorns, and, sighing in relief, Luana and Isabella let go of Nona's hands. Nona picks up her magic ball of yarn and places it back in her satchel.

"Wait a second. I recognize that satchel!" Isabella says.

Luana and Nona both look guilty, as neither of them had told Isabella about who had actually set off the smoke bomb the night of the engagement ball.

"Nona, were *you* the one who set off the smoke bomb at the engagement ball?"

"Yes, I was."

"How could you? People could have seriously gotten hurt!"

"Nona was just jealous of the princess and Lady Isabella's relationship and engagement. You know the law, Isla. No spell caster can marry a royal, and no royal can marry a spell caster."

"That doesn't seem fair...or right." Isla says.

"That's the way things have been since the founding of Gnypso."

"Can't you...I mean, can't Princess Luana change the law once she's queen?"

"I suppose she could, if enough people believed in the cause."

"I see."

Once it starts getting dark, the three girls come upon a forest and dismount.

"Why don't we set up camp, eat, and go to sleep? Who knows what we'll be facing tomorrow?" Nona asks.

Luana and Isabella agree and Nona starts setting up the only three-person tent she could find in the castle's camping storage unit.

"Need any help, Nona?" Luana asks.

"No, I've got it. Thank you, though. Why don't you girls get the starberries, raspberries, cheese and bread I packed in the cooling compartment of my satchel?"

The two girls nod and they take out the food from Nona's satchel and set the containers on a blanket that Nona had packed.

Nona soon pitches the tent and starts a fire.

"Excuse me? Is someone there?" A male voice calls out before the girls start to eat.

"Hello?" Luana replies, starting to get up. Nona yanks her back down.

"Louisa, what are you doing? We don't know who that is. For all we know, they could be against us." Nona whisper screams at Luana.

"We won't know unless we talk to them, Nona." Luana says before getting up.

"Hello? Is someone out there?" Luana exclaims.

"Yes!"

The voice, belonging to a young man with black hair, fair skin and green eyes limps towards the girls' camp.

"He has a limp!" Luana observes.

"You two must make a perfect match then." Nona replies sarcastically.

"Please...I've been wandering for days, without food or water or shelter. Could you perhaps spare some food?"

Nona eyes the young man warily.

"How do we know we can trust you?"

"Please, ma'am, I am just a humble and weary traveler, and I lost my horse...and my way."

"That sounds really dubious, if you ask me."

"I know it does, but I swear to the seven deities that I am telling you the absolute and honest-to-Aileen truth."

"We'll take your word for it. Come and sit." Luana says.

"What are you three ladies doing all the way out here?" The young man asks.

"We're on the quest to find the girl who spins the magic yarn."

"Ah. Maybe I could be of assistance."

"Oh?"

"I happen to know the...troubles you'll meet along the way."

"How so?"

"I haven't been on the quest myself, but I know...well, *knew,* someone who has...had."

"Knew?" Isabella asks.

"My grandfather. For some reason, the power of spell casting skipped my generation, so neither I nor any of my siblings or cousins have magic."

"Isla and I understand. I'm Louisa."

"Emmitt. Where are you ladies from?"

"Hartreusia. We, um, work for Princess Luana." Isabella responds.

"That must be quite the job, especially with the royal wedding coming up in a few months. I've never been so lucky to find myself tied down to anyone, but I hear that Princess Luana and Lady Isabella make quite the pair."

"Are you sure there's no one you'd like to spend the rest of your life with?" Luana asks, curiously.

"Well, there is this one girl...but I don't think she'd return my feelings if I were to confess mine to her. Her name is Celeste and she..." Emmitt pauses, trying to choose his next words carefully, "she means the world to me. We've been best friends since we were little, and there's nothing I wouldn't do to protect her."

"It seems like you've got quite the crush on her, Emmitt. Why haven't you told her how you feel?" Isabella asks.

"Oh, I don't know. I'm afraid it might ruin our friendship. You know, I've heard a rumor that Princess Luana is part siren."

"W-where did you hear that?"

"Oh, around the village. I'm from Hartreusia myself but moved to Lavenderia to be closer to Celeste."

"So, do you know anything about the girl who spins the magic yarn?" Nona asks.

"I haven't been on the quest myself, so, no. I know nothing about her, or where she is. Well, *almost* nothing. I just know she's the girl who spins the magic yarn to provide magic to spell casters."

"Okay. Do you live close by, Emmitt?" Luana asks.

"I live...well, *lived*, with my grandparents when my parents and most of my siblings all died in a fire. It was a horrible accident, but it left me an orphan."

"You say you *lived* with your grandparents. Are they dead?"

"Nona!"

"No, it's okay, Louisa. Yes, unfortunately, they did die. It was a pack of rabid elves."

"Rabid elves?"

"I was out for the day, so I didn't see them get killed...but it was horrible, nonetheless."

"I'll bet it was. We're so sorry you had to go through that." Isabella says.

"Thank you. But enough about me. What about you ladies?"

"Isla and I are both from Rosiary, and Louisa was born and raised in Hartreusia." Nona says.

"Are you and Isla sisters or cousins or...?"

"Nope. The three of us are just really close friends. It's thanks to Louisa here that we have that job working for Princess Luana. If it weren't for her, we'd probably both be living on the streets."

"I see. So, you said you work closely with Princess Luana."

"We do. We're her ladies-in-waiting." Luana says.

"Gotcha. It must be hard being ladies-in-waiting, not being royals, but not being commoners either."

"It...can be hard at times. But we get through it." Nona says.

"What I wouldn't give to see the inside of a castle one day."

"We could always take you back with us." Isabella says.

"Oh, no. Hartreusia may not be that far, but it's much too far from Celeste. I couldn't abandon her. Not after everything she's been through, losing her parents and being raised by her grandmother back when she was little."

"We're so sorry she went through that. I lost my parents at a young age myself. It was only six years ago, when I was 11, but, still, I was young."

"I guess the three of us have that in common, Nona." Emmitt chuckles a bit.

"It's getting late, and we should probably head to bed." Luana says.

"I wish I could stay, but I'd better get back to Celeste."

"Do you want us to walk you home? Or give you one of our horses?" Isabella asks.

"Oh, thank you, but no. I can manage well on my own."

"All right. Well, be careful, and farewell, Emmitt." Nona says.

"Thank you, ladies. And good luck with the rest of your quest."

"Thank you. Good night, Emmitt." Luana says.

Emmitt departs as Nona douses the flames from the fire and heads into the tent with Luana and Isabella to go to bed.

Soon, during the middle of the night, Emmitt comes across a small house in the middle of the woods.

He knocks on the door, and a girl answers it.

"Well, Emmitt? Is it them?"

"It's them. Princess Luana is definitely recognizable with her red hair and Lady Isabella is definitely the girl with black hair. Celeste, what are you going to do to them?"

"I'm going to destroy them, Emmitt. Once and for all."

"But they seemed like fairly nice girls to me."

"That's what they *wanted* you to think, Emmitt. Don't let your guard down. Especially when we're so close to my goal: destroying that *pretty little princess* for good." Celeste sits at her table to see where the girls are now.

"What are you going to do now?"

"I'm going to keep an eye on them. You go get some rest. You can start back out again tomorrow. You did a very good job deceiving those girls, Emmitt."

"Thanks, Celeste. Good night."

"Oh, it will be. Once that precious princess is gone, the king and queen will have no choice but to bow to me."

~ Six ~

The next morning, the girls realize something.

"Emmitt never told us last night about the dangers we'll be facing." Luana says.

"It is *technically* against the law to tell the questers what dangers they'll be facing." Nona replies.

"That's another law that'll be going away once I'm queen." Luana retorts.

"Along with the age-old law that says spell casters and royals can't marry, or the one that says spell casters and non-spellers can't marry." Isabella suggests.

"Exactly."

"Girls, as fun as this little chat is, we need to get going so we can face the dangers head on and get through them without turning back." Nona says.

Isabella and Luana sigh and mount their horses.

Nona can't help but hear Isabella mutter "spoilsport" under her breath as she passes Nona. Nona ignores her hurtful comment, knowing that facing her troubles at this moment in time won't solve anything.

The trio heads toward a clearing, and they see a band of...something...coming towards them.

"Could it be the Dangerous Deviants?" Luana asks hopefully.

"I doubt it." Nona replies as she takes out her spyglass. Nona gasps.

"What is it, Nona?" Isabella asks.

"Orcs."

"Orcs? What are orcs?"

"Surely you've heard of orcs, Isla. They're big and dumb and they have their own magic system. But they can only use magic on each other, and not on humans."

The band of orcs comes towards the girls, and Nona prepares herself by taking out her magic ball of yarn.

"Get behind me." Nona tells the other girls.

"No way am I going down without a fight." Isabella says, taking out her bow and quiver of arrows.

The orcs get closer and the leader spots Nona's magic ball of yarn.

"Oi! 'ow's a bit o' string s'pposed to defeat us?" The leader asks.

"Well, I'll show you. Isla, Louisa, get behind me. Now." The girls do as they're told, but Isabella still has her bow and arrow at the ready.

"Lightning Basalt." Nona whispers into her palm.

A lightning bolt strikes down and kills the leader of the orcs.

"That ought to do it." Nona says, looking back and smirking at the other girls.

"Um...Nona?" Luana points at something in front of them.

The orcs aren't retreating; they're mad and out for revenge.

"You think you can kill our leader and get away with it?!" One of the orcs asks, fuming.

"Well, that's what we were hoping..." Nona says, sheepishly.

The two remaining orcs charge and Isabella starts firing arrows, one behind the other. She strikes one in the eye, and the other in the heart. The two orcs fall dead to the ground.

"Isla, that was incredible!" Nona says.

"I told you I wasn't going down without a fight!" Isabella exclaims.

"You really proved yourself. Come on. Let's get going." Nona says, patting Isabella on the shoulder as Nona passes on her horse.

"Thanks, Nona."

Nona smiles to herself. Maybe Lady Isabella isn't so bad after all, and, besides, they came from the same country.

The girls head on towards the next bit of forest when they hear a muttering and chattering coming from below them.

"Rabid elves. Girls, retreat. I'll hold them off." Isabella says, nocking another arrow.

"Like Isla said, I am *not* going down without a fight." Luana replies.

"Louisa, how are you going to fight them? You don't even have a – " Nona pauses as Luana dismounts and grabs Nona's sword and starts slashing at the rabid elves. Soon, the elves are all dead. Nona furiously dismounts, Isabella following her.

"Louisa, are you insane? You could've seriously gotten hurt, and there's no coming back from being bitten by a rabid elf, no matter how much magic power I have!" Nona shouts.

"I can handle myself out here, Nona! I'm not some damsel in distress that needs rescuing! I can do this, but I can't if you won't let me at least try!"

"If you got hurt, even just a little bit, it would be *on me*. You have no idea what I go through to make sure both you and Isla make it out of this quest without even a scratch!"

"We don't need your protection, Nona! You saw how Isla handled those orcs back there. If it weren't for her, *you* would probably be dead, and this quest would have had to stop, and then I would've had to go back and live on without my best friend."

"I thought *Isla* was your best friend, Louisa."

"She is. But so are you! You're allowed to have more than one best friend, Nona! There's no rule or law against it!"

"I – but I thought that you were...you know what? Forget it. Let's just keep going."

"Nona..."

"Just forget it, okay?"

Wordlessly, the girls climb onto their horses and move forward.

They make it to the other patch of woods, when a lightning storm hits.

"Wonder what could've caused that?" Luana says sarcastically, looking at Nona.

"If I could be of any assistance, dears."

The girls shriek as they hear an unfamiliar voice, and they look down in front of their horses. A brown-haired old woman with white skin and teal eyes is looking up at the trio.

"Sorry to frighten you ladies, but with this storm rolling in, you might want to look for shelter for the night, or at least the time being. Come, come. No need to be shy. I don't bite."

The girls cautiously follow the old woman to her small shack near a creek.

"Your horses can go out back in the old stable. There are no animals there now, but I always provide shelter, fresh hay and fresh water to any weary traveler's horse."

"Thank you. Uh, what was your name again?" Luana asks.

"I never told you. My name is Hazel."

"Hazel. Nice to meet you. I'm Louisa, and this is Nona and Isla."

"A pleasure to meet you ladies. Now, come inside and have a seat. I'll prepare my nice warm secret stew for you to chew on."

"Thank you, Hazel, but we won't be here very long. Just until the storm passes."

"Oh, Nona. Nona, Nona, Nona. Who knows how long that will take? It could take hours for the storm to pass. And what better way to pass the time than by sharing a meal with some good friends?" Hazel chuckles to herself.

The girls follow Hazel into her shack, and it's a simple little shack. The exterior is, like the tavern, brown, but it's much smaller than The Keen Couple. Hazel's hut has a thatched roof, a couple of windows out front, and a door on the side after the staircase leading up to the landing before the front door. When you walk in the door, there is a coat rack to the right of the door, and a place to the left of the door to put your shoes. Across from the front door is the small kitchen, with a black medieval-looking refrigerator and stove, though Hazel prefers to prepare her meals at the fireplace, which is on the other side of the coat rack.

Near the fireplace is a table and chairs; Hazel prefers to not have much electricity in her hut, as she desires to live off-the-grid, away from most of civilization in Lavenderia, and on Gnypso. Hazel lives alone, and she prefers it that way, although she loves having guests to feed her secret stew to.

"Well, if you insist," Nona comments.

"You two girls can take off your cloaks. No need to be in disguise around an old woman like me." Hazel tells Isabella and Luana.

Luana and Isabella eye each other guardedly with their hands on the hoods of their respective cloaks. After a few seconds, Luana and Isabella let their guard down.

"Princess! Your Ladyship!" Hazel says, curtsying.

"Oh, Hazel. There's no need to curtsy to us. We're outsiders." Luana remarks.

"But you two are *royalty*. I knew I should've recognized your voices from the moment I heard you both speak. I am honored to make your acquaintance and be in the presence of such fine two young ladies. Can't find anyone like them elsewhere, am I right, Nona?" Hazel asks, elbowing Nona in the back as Nona hangs up the girls' cloaks.

"We still need to keep a low profile. Who knows what could be lurking out there waiting for us to put our guard down?"

"I can tell you one thing, Nona. My home is protected by magic. The weary travelers who come here have all been spell casters or friends or family of spell casters, and all of those travelers that have stayed here have cast a protection spell on it, and it lasts quite a long time. I'd say for half a millennium, give or take a few years."

"Half a millennium? Hazel, how old – "

"Tut, tut, tsk, tsk, tsk. You should never ask a lady her age, Isabella. Surely you know that, being a lady yourself."

"Well, I – "

"Oops! Soup's ready, ladies!" Hazel says, going over to her stove.

"But, Hazel..." Luana starts.

"Hmm?"

"I thought we were having stew."

"Soup, stew. Whatever you want to call it, it's hot and it's filled with good eating."

The three girls chuckle at each other as Hazel fills four bowls with good-smelling stew.

"What's in this?" Nona asks.

"Well, if I told you, it wouldn't be my *secret* stew, now would it? Eat up, Nona, before the stew gets chilled."

The four women begin to eat the stew, and it's got a very good, albeit gamey, flavor. It's got raspberries and starberries, along with exotic spices and carrots, potatoes and green beans, and a meat that Isabella, Nona and Luana can't quite place.

It's surprisingly delicious.

After the group of women eat, they notice the storm raging outside.

"Oh, my. I hope no one gets caught in that storm." Hazel says.

As soon as Hazel says that, there's a pounding at the door, and all of the girls – excluding Hazel – shriek in surprise.

"I'll get it! It could be another weary traveler come to join us. I'll be just a minute, ladies."

"No, Hazel, don't!" Nona whispers. She grabs Hazel from behind and ducks behind the door.

"Please. I am but a weary traveler, come to seek shelter from the storm."

"It's Emmitt!" Isabella whispers.

Nona lets go of Hazel and opens the door, letting Emmitt in.

"Oh, thank the seven deities." Emmitt murmurs.

"Uh, you're welcome." Nona says sarcastically, waiting for Emmitt to say thank you to her for letting him in the home.

"Oh, where are my manners? Thank you...Nona? What are you and the others doing here?"

"Same as you, Emmitt. Seeking shelter from the storm."

"I see. Well, is there any of that delicious-smelling stew left?"

"How'd you know it was stew?" Nona asks, suspicious of Emmitt.

"I may have been outside the door for quite some time, but I didn't want to intrude on your supper, ladies. I apologize for eavesdropping."

"Oh, come sit down. Warm yourself by the fire." Hazel says, grabbing Emmitt by the arm and sitting him in front of the fire, wrapping him in a blanket and handing him a bowl of stew.

"It seems the limp in your leg has gotten much better, Emmitt." Luana says.

"My – my what?"

"Your leg?"

"Oh, right. Yeah, it seems to have healed itself."

"If only that were true." Nona mutters.

"Now, now, Nona. It's not polite to mutter. What did you say to our guest?" Hazel asks.

"I said...I *asked* how do you like the stew?"

"It's quite nice, to be honest. Nice and hot, flavorful. I'll have to get the recipe so I can make it for myself and Celeste."

"Celeste? How is the old girl, Emmitt?"

"Oh, she's fine. Temperamental, but fine, Hazel."

Nona draws her sword and points it under Emmitt's chin.

"How'd you know Hazel's name?"

"Didn't she," Emmitt clears his throat, "didn't she tell me?"

"No, she didn't. Who are you, Emmitt? If that even is your real name." Luana asks.

"Well, *Princess*. I work for Celeste. She's been spying on you through me since I first spotted you gals in The Keen Couple." Emmitt says.

"What kind of...what does Celeste want with us?"

"What she's always wanted. Revenge for letting Nona take her place as your friend, *Your Highness*. Instead of being – " Emmitt stops short, not willing to finish his sentence.

"Instead of being *what*, Emmitt?" Isabella asks.

"Your Ladyship. Luana I knew would accompany Nona on her quest, but *you*? It's no secret that Nona despises you." Emmitt says, bowing mockingly.

"Despises me? For what reason?"

"Because you took her place. As Luana's – that is, *Princess* Luana's – best friend and love interest. It seems like Celeste is getting her wish after all, Nona, with you feeling the pain she's felt all of these years for *you* taking *her* place as Princess Luana's best friend."

"Does Celeste know you're spilling all of her secrets?" Nona inquires.

"Oh, I have but one secret left, but I won't tell you. I've had my fair share of scrapes and bruises from Celeste, but they're *nothing* compared to the revenge she'll dish out to you and Princess Luana. After all, revenge is a dish best. Served. Cold." Emmitt says menacingly.

"Emmitt...you don't have to do this. You can still be good. Celeste doesn't know how kind and considerate you are." Luana pleads.

"It was all a ruse! A ruse to get you to trust me, so I could lure you to her! So the world could be rid of the princess who rejected her, and of the girl who took her place as the princess' best friend."

"What about Isabella?" Nona asks.

"Oh, thank you for reminding me, Nona. She will be sent back to tell King Carter and Queen Juniper that their daughter is dead. That Princess Luana was rightfully killed to get revenge for the friendship that never was."

"You may be working for a villain, Emmitt, but you don't have to do that anymore. You can change. You can be good."

"What difference does it make?! It's not like Celeste could ever love someone like me! I'm just her obedient servant, made to do her bidding while she sits in her cottage and spies on the people who did her wrong." Emmitt says, defeated.

"Tell us where Celeste is, and do it now, before I run you through." Nona threatens, placing her sword's tip on Emmitt's chest.

"Honestly, Nona, you'd be doing me and Celeste quite the favor. You'd be saving her the job of killing me herself."

"Why would she kill you?" Isabella asks.

"Because I betrayed her. And...I'm about to betray her again."

Emmitt takes out a dagger and gouges out his own eyeballs, making him blind. He screams in agony. Luana vomits.

"Emmitt, why...what did you...?" Nona asks, almost speechless.

"I did it so she can't see what I'm doing." Emmitt starts tearlessly crying. "I never meant to hurt you girls. You've shown me nothing but kindness and compassion from the moment we met. And here I am, betraying the few people who have shown me kindness. I can only hope you can find it in your hearts to forgive me."

"Emmitt...you sacrificed your sight just so Celeste wouldn't be able to find us. That's the greatest sacrifice anyone has ever made for us. Thank you." Luana says, hugging Emmitt.

"I am so sorry, Princess. If I can do *anything* to repay you for your kindness towards me, name it, and it's yours." Emmitt says, hugging Luana back.

"Take us to Celeste, so we can make this right. Please." Isabella says.

"I know the way like I know the back of my hands. I could do it blindfolded...although, now that I think about it, doing it blindfolded would be pointless, considering I'm now blind." Emmitt chuckles, and the girls chuckle along with him.

"Come on. I'll take you to her."

After getting a pair of sunglasses for Emmitt, and a short goodbye to Hazel and thanking her for her hospitality, Emmitt, now changed, stumbles out of Hazel's shack and out into the wilderness, ready to lead his new friends to his former crush and former best friend.

~ Seven ~

"You do realize, in this situation, it's the literal blind leading the figuratively blind? What if he's luring us into a trap?" Isabella quietly asks.

"Well, if that were the case, would Emmitt have gouged out his own eyes?" Nona asks.

"Good point, Nona."

Emmitt trips a few times on the way to Celeste's, but he manages to lead the girls there.

"On the way back, one of you could have me behind you while you – I mean, *we* – ride back to Hartreusia. I probably won't be much help back at the castle, but I'm sure you could find *something* for me to do."

"After you sacrificed your sight for us, it would be my honor to find you a job that doesn't require sight. Do you have any experience in doing anything?" Luana asks.

"I love to bake...or I *did*, when I could see."

Isabella perks up at this.

"You can still bake, you know. One of the bakers at the castle is actually legally blind, and I'm sure she could help guide you."

"That would be great, Nona. Thank you so much."

"You're welcome. Oh...let me wipe the blood from your face." Nona says, taking out a clean rag from her satchel.

"I thought I felt something, and I thought it was blood, but I couldn't ask any of you ladies to do it for me."

"Why?"

"Because I'm a gentleman."

"That doesn't mean we can't help you."

"You've got me there, Isabella."

"Emmitt, take my arm above my elbow. It's right near your chest." Emmitt takes Nona's arm above her elbow.

"And there's a rock you can sit on right in front of you. Just turn around and sit." Nona instructs.

"Thank you." Emmitt sits on the rock and Nona kneels before him, gently taking his face and wiping the blood from it. When she finishes wiping the blood from Emmitt's face, she helps him up and he takes her arm again.

"We really need to get you a cane or a guide dog."

"Are you saying you don't enjoy my company?" Emmitt asks slyly and jokingly.

"No. Just saying that, once we get back to the castle, I'll have princess duties to attend to, being the princess' lady-in-waiting and best friend – well, *one* of her best friends, anyway!" Nona says, looking back and winking at Luana and Isabella.

"Can't argue with that logic. What's in front of us?" Emmitt wonders.

"River rapids." Luana says, stepping up beside Emmitt.

"How are we going to get across?" Emmitt inquires.

"We'll use a rope. Emmitt, you'll be holding my hand and I will tell you exactly where to place which foot. We have to trust each other, okay?" Nona appeals.

"I wouldn't be here if it weren't for you girls, and I mean that in the best way possible. I trust you gals." Emmitt proudly and confidently declares.

"Good. We'll tie ropes around each of our waists, and I'll lead us. We all need to trust each other and be careful. We can do this. I believe in us."

"I believe in us, too." Emmitt says.

"We believe in us and each other as well." Luana says.

"Agreed." Isabella says.

"Okay. Let's get going." Nona says, taking out a thick rope from her satchel. She makes an autoblock knot and ties the rope around each of her companions and then herself. Emmitt takes her hand.

"Okay, Emmitt. Put your left foot forward and about an inch to your left." Emmitt does what he's told, and his foot finds the first rock.

"I've got you. Bring your right foot forward and place it next to your left foot." Emmitt does as instructed, and both of his feet are placed firmly on the first rock.

With that system going strongly, the group of four slowly but surely make it across the river rapids.

"We did it. We really did it! High five!" Emmitt rejoices, holding his hand up. Nona high fives him, and begins to untie the ropes from Emmitt, Isabella, Luana and herself.

"Now what?" Isabella asks, coming to stand by Emmitt.

"Well, let me see what's ahead. Emmitt, Isabella is to your left." Nona announces.

"Got it. Thanks, Nona. Thank you, Lady Isabella." Emmitt says, taking Isabella's arm.

"Just Isabella is fine, Emmitt."

"Alright then, Isabella."

Nona disappears into the trees and comes back out a few minutes later.

"What's out there, Nona?" Luana asks.

"A field of poisonous flowers."

"What is it with the open fields and dangerous obstacles?" Emmitt queries.

"I have no idea, Emmitt." Isabella replies.

"How can you tell that they're poisonous just by looking at them?" Luana asks.

"They're Atropa belladonna, otherwise known as –"

" – Deadly Nightshade." Emmitt finishes for her.

"How'd you know that?" Isabella questions.

"I know flowers, some of which are beautiful but deadly, and some of which are beautiful and safe." Emmitt answers.

"We'll have to keep that in mind." Nona states.

"Well, Nona, how are we going to get across them this time? Should we go back and get the horses?" Luana asks.

"I can smell a storm coming, guys, and there wouldn't be time to go back to get the horses *and* make it across the field before the storm hits." Emmitt explains.

"Then we'll just have to use the spell to make us impervious again." Isabella suggests.

"Good thinking, Isabella." Nona praises.

"Thanks, Nona."

"Alright. Emmitt, you okay with being on Isabella's arm?"

"No problem."

Nona says the "Abracadabra" spell as she and the others lock hands, with Emmitt being on Isabella's arm with his left hand and holding Luana's left hand with his right, with Nona on Luana's right.

As the group walks across, Emmitt and Isabella get to talking.

"So, Emmitt, you said you're from Hartreusia originally. I've barely been there for a few weeks, and I don't really know what life is like outside the castle walls. What's it like in the village in Hartreusia?"

"It's quaint, but still, it's a good village to live in. I can still remember the layout of the village like I was there yesterday."

"Maybe you could show me around sometime?"

"It would be my pleasure to escort you around the village of Sunshire, where I grew up."

"Why, thank you, my good sir."

"You're quite welcome, my lady."

Luana and Nona have also been talking while walking across the flower field.

"So, what's the first thing you're going to do once we're back home, Princess?" Nona inquires.

"Take a long hot bath. Care to join me, Nona?" Luana asks.

"That would be a good way to relax, but, considering you're engaged to Isabella, I'm sure neither the press nor your parents and subjects would find that appropriate."

"You take the fun out of everything, Nona."

"Oh, please, I am the *queen* of fun."

"You better not say that in front of my mother, or, for that matter, in front of me! I am the future queen of Hartreusia and Gnypso, after all."

"Don't remind me."

"So, guys, what's it like back in the castle in Hartreusia?" Emmitt requests.

"It's big, and old, yet it's got electricity, hot running water, internet, and good plumbing." Luana answers.

"What's your favorite part of the castle?" Emmitt asks.

"The library." Luana, Isabella and Nona all say at the same time.

"Whoa. I never would've guessed you three ladies were so in sync."

"We aren't. We just know our Princess Luana very, very well." Nona says.

"Ah. I see. So, Princess, what's your ultimate plan for when you get back home?"

"Introduce you to the head baker, so she can teach you all she knows about the kitchen, and about baking."

"That would be fantastic, Luana! Er, I mean, *Princess* Luana."

"When we're not out in public, Emmitt, just Luana is fine."

"Thank you for letting me know, Luana."

"You're welcome. So, Emmitt, what was it like growing up with Celeste?"

Emmitt suddenly goes quiet, and Luana instantly realizes she's said the wrong thing.

The group goes quiet and walks a few feet without saying anything to one another.

"You okay, Emmitt?" Isabella asks.

"Yeah, Isa, I'm fine. It's just that – I've never realized how cruel Celeste was to me until you and your friends showed me so much kindness and compassion. I thought Celeste's behavior was normal."

"Oh, Emmitt, I'm so sorry Celeste put you through that. Her cruelty is *not* normal behavior, especially for someone as sweet and kind as you." Luana apologizes.

"Thank you, Luana. You're too kind."

"I think I can see the end in sight, guys." Nona tells the group.

"That's good. I could use a break."

"Emmitt!" Luana, Nona and Isabella all yell.

"I'm kidding, I'm kidding! Trust me, I know how this spell works." Emmitt jokes.

"Good. We can't have any missteps or mishandles. We have to be completely in sync." Nona explains.

The others nod at Nona as they make their way to the end of the poisonous flower field.

"We're almost there. As soon as we make our way to the end of the field, we can let go of each other's hands. I see a cave just up ahead." Nona observes.

"Wait, does that mean that *I* have to let go of Isabella?" Emmitt asks.

"No. Unless you'd rather end up lost and unable to find your way back to us." Nona says, slyly.

"Nope, nope! I'm good. I'd rather stick with you gals."

"Good. We could use you as bait for Celeste."

Emmitt gulps.

"She's joking." Luana says, warningly looking at Nona with a cross look on her face.

"I'd never let her use you as bait, Emmitt." Isabella remarks, quickly kissing Emmitt's cheek.

"Thank you, Isa."

"You're welcome. So, Emmitt, what kinds of things do you like to bake?"

"Oh, all kinds of things: scones, cakes, cupcakes, pies, cobblers."

"Maybe you could bake for me sometime? Or show me how to bake?"

"Yeah, I could do that for you, Isa."

"I'd like that, Emmitt."

The group soon comes to the end of the poisonous flower field and the rain starts to come down in sheets.

"Come on! The cave is just up ahead!" Nona shouts back to the group as she begins to run forward toward the cave.

Emmitt gripping Isabella's hand as hard as he can, with Luana trailing a bit behind them, they run into the cave as the rain starts to pour down in buckets.

~ Eight ~

As the group walks deeper into the cave, Emmitt asks something.

"What if there are dangerous animals in here?" Emmitt ponders, worriedly.

"I'll fight them off with my bow and arrow for you, Emmitt." Isabella answers.

"How noble of you, Isabella. Thank you." Emmitt replies.

"You're welcome, Emmitt."

The group gets to the cave, and, luckily, there are no dangerous animals to be seen or heard.

Nona starts a fire and the group gathers around it, huddling for warmth. Isabella and Emmitt are nearly inseparable, and Luana stays a bit closer to Nona than she usually has on this journey.

"So, Emmitt, what was it *really* like living in Sunshire?" Luana asks.

"It was nice; living with my grandparents was a bit challenging at times, but I got through it. Once I met Celeste, though, things started going wrong. My grandparents were killed by the rabid elves, people started going missing, and that's when I decided I would move to Lavenderia to live closer to Celeste. What's it like in Rosiary, Isabella?" Emmitt asks, curiously.

"It's nice. The castle, or should I say, *manor*, isn't as big as the castle back in Hartreusia, but it's still pretty big. We have a library like in Hartreusia's castle, as well as a garden, where we grow our own vegetables. My mum and dad believe in hard work, so we grow the vegetables ourselves instead of letting the servants do that."

"I see. What kinds of veggies do you grow?"

"All kinds: carrots, broccoli, asparagus, cucumbers, tomatoes, potatoes, green beans...anything you'd like, we can grow."

"Wow. That's amazing."

"Thanks, Emmitt."

"You're welcome. So, Luana, how are you feeling about becoming queen soon?"

"I don't believe I'm prepared for the job. After all the training my parents have put me through about running a kingdom and a country all at once, I don't know if I'm really ready."

"Well, you'll have me, as well as your parents, by your side to help you through it. And, of course, you'll have Isabella as your queen consort." Nona says.

"Right."

"Can I...can I tell you guys something?" Emmitt inquires.

"Of course, Emmitt. What's up?" Nona asks.

"Well, the thing is, Celeste isn't just the girl hellbent on revenge on you and Luana. She's – she's also the girl who spins the magic yarn."

"You couldn't have mentioned that to us earlier?!" Luana exclaims.

"I'm sorry. I just couldn't bring myself to tell you all because I thought you wouldn't need me anymore. After all, Nona *did* say you guys could use me as bait for Celeste."

"I was joking, Emmitt. I would never use one of my friends as bait, no matter how much wrongdoing they've done. True friends don't abandon each other, even when times are tough."

"Thank you, Nona. It – it means a lot to me that you'd say that. So, what's next for you? What will *you* do when you get back to the castle, Nona?"

"I'll probably just go back to doing my original duties. Question: will Celeste willingly give us the magic yarn?"

"At this point, probably not. We'd have to take it from her, and probably distribute it ourselves."

"Would we sell it or just give it out?" Isabella asks.

"We'd probably just give it out, then get Celeste to teach us how to make it ourselves."

"Would she willingly do that, or would we have to make her teach us?"

"She most likely wouldn't do it willingly, so we'd have to force or bribe her to teach us."

"Got it. So, anyway, I'll be doing my duties as the princess and future queen's lady-in-waiting, like keeping note of her activities, reading, embroidery, things like that."

"So, a lady-in-waiting is not a servant?" Emmitt asks.

"Technically, no. A lady-in-waiting is considered a friend of the princess or queen."

"I see. So, Nona, why do you live in the servants' quarters?"

"Surprisingly, Isabella, because there's no spare room for me, and I'd prefer to share a room with others instead of having a room all to myself."

"I understand now. Thank you for that useful information, Nona."

"You're welcome, Isabella."

"When we get back, I'd like to teach Emmitt all I know about baking before Hanna can get her hands on him." Isabella states.

"That's fine by me." Luana replies.

"Thank you, Luana."

Lightning strikes and thunder rumbles just outside the cave and the group jumps, startled.

"It doesn't seem like this storm is going to go anywhere soon, guys. What should we do in the meantime?" Emmitt wonders.

"Oooh, oooh, oooh! We could swap stories, maybe!" Isabella suggests.

"That's a good idea. Who should start?" Emmitt replies.

"I will. This one time, when Luana and I were little, and we were together, about eight or so, we were playing in the throne room, and this dog ran in, barking and wagging its tail, with a stick in its mouth. It ran over to Luana, and she was a bit scared of the dog at first, but I coaxed it over to me, and I let it smell my hand so it would know I wasn't scared of it or going to harm it. It sniffed me, and it started licking me. Luana, would you like to tell what happened next?"

"Sure, Nona. Nona threw the stick and the dog went to go fetch it, and the dog brought it over to me. Nona told me to go on and throw it for the dog, and I did, and the dog fetched the stick and brought it back to me and barked while wagging its tail. Thus, began the game of back-and-forth fetch with the dog between Nona and me. It ended when my parents found us in the throne room the next morning, and the three of us were asleep, and they all but threw the dog out because it could've wandered in from the village."

"That's quite the story. It reminds me of the time I had a cat that would bring me dead mice as a kid, back when I was living with my grandparents. It wasn't my cat, to begin with, but it was friendly, and brought me dead mice nearly every day." Emmitt states.

The group laughs at this.

"You know what would be nice right now?" Isabella asks.

"Hazel's Secret Stew?" Luana asks.

"Exactly. I couldn't quite guess what the meat was, but, at that point, it was too good for me to care." Isabella asks.

"I wish we had the recipe. I could make it for all of us." Emmitt says.

"Yeah, and you'd probably end up chopping your fingers off in the process." Isabella teases.

"Hey! I do have *some* cooking skills, even though baking is my forte."

"Baking is a science, where you have to do everything exactly by the book. Cooking is a bit more experimental, where you can add a little bit of this and a little bit of that, and it'll turn out delicious. But baking? If you add too much flour, it'll become too doughy, or too much sugar, and it'll be way too sweet." Luana says.

"You do make a good point. How do you know so much about cooking and baking, Luana? You grew up with people to do those things for you." Emmitt says.

"When I was little, I used to help the cooks and bakers in the kitchen on special occasions, like my parents' birthdays or anniversary."

"Ah. That makes sense."

"Anyway, who's next? We've all told stories except for you, Isabella." Emmitt realizes.

"Oh. I guess I'm up next, then. Let's see. I was eleven when my little sister died. She died because a carriage ran over her. Neither my parents nor I have been the same ever since, and neither my father nor my mother have had a drink since, because it was a drunk driver that ran Dawn over. The doctors said she died instantly, so they say she didn't feel any pain when she died."

"We are so sorry." Emmitt says, placing a hand on Isabella's arm.

"Thank you. It was six years ago, but it still hurts."

"Of *course* it still hurts, Isabella. Dawn was your sister." Nona says.

"I – I was told to not tell anyone about Dawn or her death, like it would dishonor her memory. But I couldn't keep it inside any longer."

"Thank you for telling us about Dawn. Maybe someday you could tell us more about her."

"Once we get back home, I will."

"All four of us?" Emmitt asks.

"Of course, silly!" Luana says.

Nona wanders to the edge of the cave.

"I think the storm has passed." Nona calls back.

"I'll douse the fire." Emmitt pauses, "I can feel you all looking at me. I'm just kidding, you know."

"Right. *I'll* douse the fire." Luana says, taking her canteen and pouring a little bit of water over the flames, extinguishing them.

"Come on, guys. I'll take to you to Celeste, so we can end this. Once and for all." Emmitt says, getting up and taking Isabella's arm.

The group walks out of the cave, and they go forward towards Celeste.

As they're walking for a while, they try to come up with a plan.

"So, what's the plan? Do we take her by surprise?" Luana asks.

"She'll be expecting that. The best thing to do is to sneak in from the back and catch her from behind." Emmitt remarks.

"So, we *do* take her by surprise?" Nona inquires.

"We have to do something unexpected, and she won't expect us to go from the back."

"Good plan, Emmitt." Isabella agrees.

"Thanks, Isa. Can we stop? I'm kind of getting tired." Emmitt suggests.

"Sounds like a good idea to me." Isabella remarks.

The group heads over to a cliff's edge and stares out at the sunset.

"Part of me wishes I hadn't gouged my eyes out. Are we looking at the sunset?"

"Yeah."

"Can – can you describe it to me, Isabella?"

"Of course, Emmitt. It's warm, and it's bright and it's lighting up the sky in all of these different colors like orange and pink and purple. It's like...hugging someone and not letting go, like hugging a friend or a loved one."

"Thank you for describing the sunset to me as if I've never seen it before. I think, when I could see, I took sunsets for granted. I only watched them when I had the time when I was little, and I never once took them in like I'm doing now."

Isabella lays her head on Emmitt's shoulder.

"You okay, Isa?"

"The fact that you gave up your sight just so Celeste wouldn't be able to find us. That means more to us than you know, Emmitt. Thank you."

"You're welcome."

"We'll never be able to repay you for what you've done for us."

"There's no need, Luana. As long as I've got you guys, I'll be okay. That being said, if things go south once we get to

Celeste, I'd sacrifice my life just so you girls would make it out alive."

Isabella begins to sob.

"Isabella?"

"I can't stand the thought of losing you, Emmitt. It would destroy me."

"I'll try my hardest to make sure that you don't lose me. I'll fight with all I've got to make sure we *all* make it out of this alive."

"No offense, Emmitt, but how will you fight when you can't see?"

"It may sound surprising, but I have impressive archery skills, and I saw your skills as well, Isabella. If we could make a bow and I could borrow some of your arrows, Isa, I'd be more than happy to fight alongside you."

"It would be my pleasure to make a bow for you, Emmitt."

"Thank you, plenty, m'lady." Emmitt grabs Isabella's hand as gently as possible (for he felt it on his lap), and he kisses it.

"I think we've had an abundance of a break. Should we keep going and try to find a branch to make into a bow for Emmitt along the way to Celeste's?" Luana asks, getting up. Isabella helps Emmitt to stand and walk away from the edge of the cliff.

"Sounds like a plan." Emmitt says.

"Let's get going then." Nona says.

The four walk into the forest leading up to Celeste's cottage, and Luana and Nona each pick up good-sized branches for Emmitt to feel and for Isabella to inspect to see if it would make a good bow, and, soon, after six failed attempts to find a good branch, they find one on the seventh try.

"I have some extra string to tie on the bow." Isabella says, going into her satchel and taking out a long bowstring.

"Why, thank you, m'lady."

"You're welcome."

Isabella makes a bow and places it over Emmitt's back and hands him her extra quiver and some arrows.

"Thank you, Isabella. I don't want to really hurt Celeste, but if it's between her and us, I'll do whatever it takes to protect us."

"Good plan, Emmitt." Nona says, punching Emmitt lightly on the shoulder.

"Thanks, Nona. Come on. I can smell the smoke coming from her chimney from here. We're getting closer." Emmitt reports.

The group moves forward, not knowing what they'll be facing next in this quest, whether it be Celeste herself or more challenges along the way to Celeste.

Soon, they take another break, and reach a clearing with a small forest in front of them.

"We're in a clearing, so we might face more dangers, but I'm praying to the seven deities that we don't." Isabella remarks.

"We could get into some target practice, if that's alright with you gals." Emmitt suggests.

"Fine by me, Emmitt. But what are we going to use as targets?" Nona asks.

"Are there any dying trees around? I'd rather not hit any living ones if I can help it." Emmitt says.

"There's a patch of them up ahead, and I can see another clearing beyond them from here." Luana observes.

"Good. My range is pretty far, even though I can't see. Just point me in the right direction, Isa."

"Can do."

Emmitt takes an arrow and nocks it, and aims at a dying tree straight ahead.

"There's a dying tree straight ahead. You're right on target."

Emmitt pulls back the arrow to his cheek, and lets it go.

He hits it right in the middle of the dying tree trunk.

"You got it!"

"I hit it? I actually hit it?"

"You sure did!"

"Watch out, Celeste! You've got nothing on us! The – the...should we come up with a name for ourselves?"

"That's not a bad idea. How about The Big Four?"

"Nah, too obvious. Besides, only half of us are royals and the other half are commoners, and it would make more sense if we were all royals. We need to come up with something good. Like, like, Lunoemisa?"

"What is *that*?" Nona asks.

"It's the first part of our names combined. No? Not good enough. You're right."

"It's not bad, but it's not...what we're looking for, Emmitt. Why don't we think up names along the way to Celeste's, and, on the way back to Hartreusia, we speak our ideas to each other?" Luana suggests.

"Good idea. Oh, I've got one more idea: Teenage Royal Commoner Squad, or the Royal Commoner Squad?"

Emmitt pauses, and joins in when the others say –

"Nah."

"Come on. We need to get to Celeste and defeat her before she knows what's coming." Nona states.

The group soon arrives at a stone-covered cottage in the forest.

"What's in front of us?"

"A cottage. And there's smoke coming out of the chimney." Isabella observes.

"This is the place. Celeste always has the fireplace going, no matter what the season is."

"Does she ever stop working?" Luana asks.

"Nope, and she rarely sleeps. She has coffee to keep her going when she gets weary."

"That's not very healthy." Isabella mutters, but loud enough so the others can hear her.

"I know. But Celeste is a stubborn gal." Emmitt says.

"I was wondering why I couldn't see where you were anymore, Emmitt." A woman with brown hair, hazel eyes, and tan skin walks out of the cottage.

"Celeste."

"Is that all you have to say to me, Emmitt? But I thought we were friends."

"We *were* friends, Celeste, until I learned that the way you've been treating me is not the way you should treat another human being."

"That *hurts*, Emmitt. I only treated you the way you *deserved* to be treated." Celeste says. It's then she notices the girls.

"Oh, and who do we have here? Princess Luana, Lady Isabella and...someone I don't recognize. A pleasure to make your acquaintance, Your Highness. Your Ladyship."

"We know how you treated Emmitt, and we know that *you're* the girl who spins the magic yarn. I'm just here to replenish my magic, and then we'll be out of your way." Nona says.

"You mustn't leave so soon! We're just getting started." Celeste suddenly pulls a lever, and Emmitt and Isabella are captured in a net.

Celeste grabs Luana and forces her inside, but not before turning to Nona.

"You, I'll give a ten-minute head start to get back to the castle in Hartreusia to tell the king and queen I have their daughter and future daughter-in-law. They'll have to pay me one million zikapia before midnight. Oh, and I'll be sending the Dangerous Deviants after you."

"But they said – "

"It was a trick. A scam. A ruse. Whatever you want to call it, they tricked you into thinking they were on *your* side. Come now, Princess. Time to send good old Mum and Dad a message." Celeste begins to drag Luana into the cottage.

"Nona! If I don't make it – "

"Oh, precious child. I'll make *sure* you don't make it. Nona, you're wasting precious time here. Tick, tock. Tick...tock." Celeste says, waving her finger at Nona.

~ Nine ~

Meanwhile, up in the net, Emmitt and Isabella are talking about what they want in life.

"So, Isabella, do you think you're ready to become the queen consort of Hartreusia and Gnypso?"

"To be honest, not really. I'm only here – well, I was only a suitor because my parents wanted to marry me off to the princess."

"That seems really cruel, marrying you off to someone you barely know."

"I know...but I didn't have any choice in the matter."

"You should be free to make your own choices, and marry whomever you want, not someone you barely know. No offense to Luana, of course."

"Maybe things could be different once Luana becomes queen...but, according to tradition, divorce isn't a thing in royalty. At least on Gnypso, anyway. So, maybe things *can't* be different, even though, once she's queen, she can have power that others don't. So, who knows what'll happen once she's queen? She and I could get a divorce, and she and I could marry whomever we please. I mean, sure, *I* was the one who proposed to her, but I think she used her siren powers on me, so there's no telling how she'd react to me breaking up with –"

Emmitt suddenly kisses Isabella.

"You talk too much." Emmitt whispers to her.

"Is that a bad thing?"

"Not at all. But, to be honest, I'd rather be kissing you than talking to you. After all, out of the three of you girls, you're the most beautiful to me."

"I am?"

"You are. Inside *and* out."

"Why, thank you, Emmitt."

"You're quite welcome, Isa."

Celeste ties Luana up in a chair next to the fireplace, and it's then Luana gets a good look at Celeste's cottage.

Near the fireplace is the spinning wheel and a pile of magic yarn, with a chair in front of it, so Celeste can rest her weary self, should she need to or run out of coffee. Celeste only makes trips to the market if she needs to, when she needs food or coffee or other drinks. Across the room from the fireplace is the dining table and four chairs, and a small kitchen, a bit bigger than Hazel's. There's a small TV with a couch in the living room between the kitchen and the fireplace. The exterior of Celeste's cottage is stone and has a shingled roof.

Who comes over to keep Celeste company besides Emmitt? Luana wonders.

"Where do you even *get* the materials for magic yarn, anyway?"

"Ah, ah, ah. That's an old family secret. Nothing that concerns you, Luana." Celeste says, leaning in to Luana.

"Now, let's get to recording that message for dear old Mum and Dad. And, action!" Celeste says as she points a camera in Luana's face.

"You can't be serious."

"Must we do this the hard way, Luana?" Celeste takes out a dagger and presses it against Luana's neck.

"Now, Luana, you must cooperate."

"Mum, Dad! Don't come looking for me! Celeste is the girl who spins the magic yarn, and she's hellbent on getting revenge on me for Nona taking her place as my friend!"

"Oh, dear. She's not very compliant, is she, *Your Majesties*? Let's try that again, shall we? Take two, and, action!"

"Mum...Dad...it's Luana. Please, just stay where you are, and don't blame Nona for this. The only one here to blame is...me." Tears start falling down Luana's cheeks.

"Awww." Celeste pouts mockingly.

"If I had just explained to you that I wanted to marry Nona and not Isabella...or any royal suitor for that matter, this never would have happened. Nona wouldn't have gotten jealous, and then you wouldn't have forced the three of us to go on this quest; it would have been just Nona on the quest. So, blame *me*, punish *me*. But don't blame or punish Nona. I love you, and I'm sorry."

"Now, *that* just brings a tear to your eye, doesn't it, Lu? I think that just about covers what your parents need to hear from their precious little girl. Now, let's have some fun." Celeste sends the video to King Carter and Queen Juniper.

~.~

Meanwhile, Nona has made it back to Hartreusia on horseback, and is now approaching the king and queen.

"Ah, Nona! Found the girl already? We didn't expect you to be back so soon. Where are Princess Luana and Lady Isabella?" King Carter asks.

"That's the thing, Your Majesty. Celeste has them."

"Alright, and who is Celeste?" Queen Juniper inquires.

"Celeste is the girl who spins the magic yarn, Your Highness. She's holding Princess Luana and Lady Isabella hostage, and she sent me back to warn you and for you to give a ransom."

"What's the ransom?"

"One million zikapia."

"We can pay it immediately. Thank you for telling us."

"You're welcome, Your Majesty. Is there anything further I can do?"

"I don't believe so, Nona. Thank you."

"Of course, Your Majesty."

Nona turns to leave, but King Carter gets a notification on his tablet.

"There's a video message. It's Luana!" King Carter observes.

King Carter presses play and allows Queen Juniper and Nona to view the video with him.

"Mum...Dad...it's Luana. Please, just stay where you are, and don't blame Nona for this. The only one here to blame is...me." Tears start falling down Luana's cheeks.

"Awww." Celeste says from behind the camera.

Luana explains how she wanted to marry Nona and not Isabella, and how, if Nona hadn't gotten jealous, the three of them wouldn't have been forced to go on the quest.

"Now, *that* just brings a tear to your eye, doesn't it, Lu? I think that just about covers what your parents need to hear from their precious little girl. Now, let's have some fun." Celeste ends the video there.

"Your Majesties, you need to pay that ransom."

"We will, Nona. Go get the royal guard and get yourself ready. You'll need to lead the battalion to Celeste, and bring our Luana back home." Queen Juniper orders.

"Right away, Your Majesty." Nona curtsies and runs out to get the head of the royal guard.

Back with Emmitt and Isabella, Emmitt suddenly gasps.

"What?"

"I just remembered I still have my dagger with me. It should be in my front left pocket. Can you grab it?"

"Yes, of course. But why?" Isabella asks as she fishes around in Emmitt's front left pocket for the dagger.

"Isabella, I need you to cut your way out of this net. Leave and go get help."

"What about you?"

"I'll be fine; I can handle Celeste, but you need to get out of here and get help."

"Are you sure, Emmitt? I don't want to leave you."

"I'll be alright, Isabella. Don't worry about me. Just worry about going to get help."

Isabella grabs Emmitt by his chin and kisses him.

"In case I don't come back." Isabella tells him, mournfully.

"I hope you do, Isa. It's been a delight knowing such a lovely lady."

"Thank you. It's been quite the pleasure knowing such a fine gentleman."

"Until you return, my lady. Will you give me your hand?" Emmitt asks. Isabella complies and Emmitt kisses the back of her hand.

"Now get to cutting. We don't have much time. If Celeste kills Luana, all hell will break loose. The kingdoms will go to war, saying the kingdom of Lavenderia is to blame, and then...well, Rosiary will join the fight, then Eburnean, and then Indigonia. But I don't know who will be on whose side. My history is a bit rubbish."

"That's okay." Isabella starts cutting the net and, eventually, she jumps down from it, and Emmitt waves at her from the net. She begins to wave back, but then stops herself, remembering that Emmitt can't see her.

~.~

Isabella runs through the forest to Hazel's, and grabs her horse, knowing she's fast.

"Come on, Lexi! Let's get back home to Hartreusia. Hyah!"

Isabella and Lexi gallop back to Hartreusia in about three hours, and they reach the castle gates.

"Open the gate!"

"Isabella?"

"Nona?"

The royal guards open the gates and Isabella gallops in just as Nona and the royal guards are heading out.

"Nona? Where are you going?"

"To save Luana! Stay here with your parents and the king and queen."

"Nona, if you see Emmitt, tell him I'm alright."

"Will do, Isa! We'll be back soon!"

As the royal battalion leaves, with Nona at the head, Isabella hopes, wishes, and prays to the seven gods and goddesses that everything – and every*one* – will turn out alright.

~.~

Nona and the royal guard head forward to Lavenderia.

"We can't stop for anything, not even food or water. And, no matter what we come across, keep going. Fight with everything you've got, and don't hold back."

The royal guards nod at Nona and at each other, knowing very well that what they're going to be facing is something none of the guards have ever dealt with before.

Richard, the head of the royal guard, rides up beside Nona.

"Nona, about putting you in the dungeon. I'm – "

"Richard, you did what was protocol. No one can blame you for that. Not even me."

"Still, Nona, you should've been given a fair trial, instead of just being placed in the dungeon for the night."

"I forgive you, Richard. But there's nothing for you to apologize for."

"Thank you, Nona. Your forgiveness means a lot to me."

"You're welcome."

The battalion – with Nona and Richard at the lead – get through the trials Nona remembers facing just hours ago, the men slashing at the field of thorns and poisonous flower fields.

"You needn't waste your magic on something that can be handled with a blade, Nona." Richard tells her. Nona only smirks at the captain.

They keep going, and eventually reach Hazel's hut, and something good-smelling is coming out from the windows.

"What is that delicious smell?" One of the men asks.

"Keep your focus, men. Don't get distracted, no matter how delicious the source of that smell...smells..." Richard says.

The group keeps going and gets past Hazel's hut, and eventually, they make it to the cliff where Nona remembers she and the others watched the sunset. It's nearly midnight now.

"What I wouldn't give for a cup of coffee right now." Herbert remarks. The other soldiers agree with him.

Nona rides forward and stops before the men.

"Come on, guys, we need to focus. Princess Luana's life is at stake here, and we can't afford any distractions." Nona says.

"She's right!" A voice says from above Nona.

"Emmitt!"

"Hey, Nona."

"Isabella, that is *Lady* Isabella, wanted me to tell you that she's alright."

"I am glad to hear it. I'd offer to help, but, being fully blind, I don't think I'd be of much assistance."

"Good call, Emmitt. We'll rescue Luana and then we'll cut you down."

"Take your time. I'm not going anywhere."

Nona and the guard go towards the door to Celeste's cottage, prepared for the unexpected.

~ Ten ~

"Celeste, please don't do this. You can be the better person here."

"No, I can't, Princess."

"If you want, you could join our group, and we could keep your secret."

"Which secret?"

"The secret that you're the girl who spins the magic yarn."

"Oh, please. I'm sure your precious...whoever she is...told the king and queen of my true identity."

"How do you know that?"

"Because I see all, and I know all."

"How?"

"By looking through others' eyes."

"That seems pretty invasive."

"It's not. It's quite simple, really." Celeste suddenly sputters.

"Why am I telling you and having a pretty little chat with you, like we're having afternoon tea?" Celeste asks.

"I don't know. You tell me. You're the one who brought up Nona telling the king and queen about your real identity."

"Look, Princess. I don't *care* about my secret identity."

"So *why* do you work so hard to erase people's memories of you?"

"Because I want what you have. Power. And I'd have that power if you had fallen for *me* instead of that stupid lady-in-waiting of yours."

"You're doing all this because I paid attention to Nona and not to you?"

"Exactly!"

"That's pretty pathetic if you ask me."

"I'm not pathetic!"

"I never said *you* were pathetic. I just said your reasons for holding me hostage are pretty pathetic."

"Same difference! See here, Princess, if you had just talked to me, you wouldn't be here begging for your life."

"Um, I don't see me begging here." Luana says, smirking at Celeste.

"Do you want me to *make* you beg for mercy?"

"No. I just want you to let me go, and we won't turn you in."

"Oh, *you* won't turn me in, but the royal battalion sure will. And do you want to know why? Because I kidnapped the crown princess of Hartreusia!"

"You could've asked for anything to trade for me, and yet you asked for money. What would you do with one million zikapia, anyway?"

"I'd...why does it matter to you what I do with that money?"

"Well, I want to know what I'm being traded for."

"It's none of your business what you're being traded for. It's my money, and I can do whatever I want with it!"

Meanwhile, Emmitt is questioning his life choices. In other words, he's having an existential crisis.

"What am I doing here? Here, in this world? Why did Celeste choose me to be her friend? Why did I never tell her how I felt? What if she *does* end up killing Luana? What then? I mean, wouldn't that give her more power than she needs? What will happen to Isabella? Would she ever fall for someone like me? A guy who used to work for Celeste?"

Emmitt continues questioning his existence, and he eventually comes up with all of the answers to the questions he had been asking himself.

"I'm here to make sure Celeste doesn't hurt Luana, even though I can't really do anything in this net. Celeste chose me to be her friend because she was lonely, and felt rejected by Luana, and I never told her how I felt because I guess I knew deep down that Celeste was trouble. If Celeste ends up killing Luana, all hell will definitely break loose, and Isabella would probably have to go back to Rosiary, and I'd probably never see her again. Not that it matters, since I don't think she cares about me the way I care about her."

At the same time, Isabella is back in Hartreusia, having questions of her own for herself.

"Why did I propose to Luana only after a week of knowing her? Why do I want to marry someone who doesn't want to marry me? It's no secret about how Luana feels about Nona. What if I objected at the wedding, and said I wanted to marry Emmitt instead? Would my parents be in such shock, they'd fall down dead, or would they be okay with me being with someone who's not a royal? I mean, it's quite possible that Emmitt and I could make a life together, despite him not being a royal. I mean, what makes a royal, anyway? Not just blood, but someone who's kind and compassionate, someone who puts others before themselves. Emmitt...he sacrificed his sight for us, just so Celeste wouldn't be able to find us."

Isabella, too, comes to the answers to the questions she asked herself.

"I only proposed to Luana, because that was what was expected of me, and I only wanted to marry her to please my parents. If I objected at the wedding, my parents would just have to deal with it. Emmitt, wherever you are, I hope you're listening to me. I don't know how you'd hear me, considering we're miles apart but I just want you to know that I – I love you, and I hope to see you soon."

Back with Celeste and Luana...

"Join me, Princess, and we can rule together, creating a world so dark, people will have no choice but to bow to us."

"Celeste, I'm not going to switch over to the dark side. It's not who I am. I'm a princess of light, not darkness."

"But I can *make* you do whatever I want. So, I can *force* you to turn over to the dark side, and join me in my quest to defeat your dear old Mum and Dad."

"Why do you hate me so much? Yes, I chose Nona instead of you, but why are you so set on killing me?"

"Because *I* was the one who gave you your limp, not Nona!"

Luana leans back, and gasps.

"What? *You* were the one who gave me my limp?"

"Let's take a mind trip back, shall we?"

Celeste places her hands on Luana's temple, and Luana is transported back to the day of the accident.

She and Nona, both twelve at the time, are playing in the courtyard of the palace, being watched carefully by the nanny and the royal guard.

Celeste and Luana, at their current ages, stand from afar, looking at the past.

"Can they see us?"

"No. We can see and hear them, but they can't see or hear us."

"Who are they? I mean, I recognize Nona, but who is that little girl with her?"

"That's you, you imbecile. Don't you see the bright red hair?"

"It's not *that* bright."

"Whatever. Let's just watch the scene unfold."

Celeste and Luana crouch behind the bushes in the courtyard, and Luana sees a young girl with tan skin, hazel eyes and brown hair peeking out from up in a tree; she had sneaked her way onto the castle grounds.

"Chase me, Nona!"

"I am, Princess!"

Little Celeste sees a large rock and places it in front of the young princess, and Luana trips as she's looking back at young Nona, and Celeste, at the same time as Nona, fires a magic beam at Luana, Nona to catch her, Celeste to let her fall.

Celeste's beam makes it before Nona's does, but neither past Nona nor past Luana notice, as Luana has too much pain in her left leg to care. She cries out in agony.

"Princess! Nona, what were you thinking?" The nanny asks, gently grabbing the princess and holding her.

"I – I thought my magic could save her."

"That's what you get for thinking, Nona! Guards, go get the king and queen. They need to have a serious talk with Nona about not using magic unless absolutely necessary."

"Right away."

"Oh, there, there, Princess. Shhh. You'll be just fine. We'll have the healer look at your leg and see what she can do." The nanny soothes.

"Luana, I – "

Young Luana shies away from young Nona, placing her face in the bosom of her nanny.

"You – you were trying to kill me then!" Current Luana exclaims to current Celeste.

"All because you didn't see me when we were younger. You could've avoided years of pain and misery if you had just paid attention to me."

"I can't believe all of this never would've happened if I had just paid attention to you when we were young children. What am I saying? I was *four* when I met Nona! I became friends with Nona because she was the first girl I laid eyes on when my parents and I visited Rosiary!"

"That's not my fault."

"But it *is* your fault that I now have a limp, *and* that you tried to kill me for something I didn't really have any control over!"

Back in the real world, Celeste lets go of Luana in frustration, not believing what she's hearing.

"Celeste, why did you show me that? Why make me relive that horrible day?"

"So you could see that it was actually me, and not your precious Nona. But we have one more time trip to make."

Celeste puts her hands on Luana's temple once again and they are transported back thirteen years, to when Luana and Nona met.

Celeste points out her past self to present Luana, looking longingly – and jealously – at the princess and Nona.

Celeste, back in reality, lets go of Luana's head and Luana's mind is transported back to reality.

"Celeste, you can cross over to the good side. I mean, look at what Emmitt did. He sacrificed his sight for us, so you wouldn't be able to see what he was doing!"

"Yes, yes, yes. He's such a big hero! Big deal! I could still see what you were doing and where you were. Like I've said, I don't only have the power to see through Emmitt's eyes, but also through others' eyes as well."

"So, you never needed Emmitt. Why keep him around for so long, then?"

"For companionship. Being the girl who spins the magic yarn, who also erases the memories of everyone who comes across her, day after day, becomes lonely."

"So, you only kept him around because you were lonely? That's...pretty relatable, to be honest."

"Oh, what do you care? You have everything you could want: a nice bed, shelter, good food."

"But I'd be nothing if I didn't have the love and support of my family and friends. You can have that, if you just simply *try*. You don't have to be the bad guy."

"I'm done trying, Princess. I've been trying all of my life to make sure you pay for all of the wrongs you've done to me."

"We could be friends, Celeste. We could start over."

"No, Princess, we can't. Because, once again, I captured the crown princess of Hartreusia, and, no matter how much magic I have, there's no going back from that!"

Celeste fires a beam at Luana, who dodges it. Celeste keeps firing, and Luana keeps dodging. There's suddenly a knock at the door.

~ Eleven ~

After knocking on the door, Nona and the royal guard wait.

"I've got a little bit of magic left. If I can take Celeste down with one hit, you guys can go in and capture her."

"And if you fail?"

"Then...we'll lure her outside."

Nona opens the door, and the sight before her surprises her.

"Stop right there!" Nona exclaims. She sees Celeste and Luana fighting each other – okay, Celeste fighting Luana with her magic, and Luana dodging her attacks. The cottage is a mess, and Luana is getting tired of dodging Celeste's attacks.

Luana crisscrosses her arms to block another attack, when, suddenly, beams shoot out from Luana's hands, breaking the mirror to her left and the window to her right.

"Time out! I have magic?"

"How is that possible?" Nona and Celeste ask, looking at each other then back at Luana.

"I don't know. But I have magic, which means I can fight back!"

Celeste puts her arms up to dodge Luana's attacks, but Luana – despite just learning she has magic – is too fast and hits Celeste with a beam of magic.

The two continue to fight, dodging each other's attacks and throwing beams of magic at each other.

"Luana!" Luana, dodging Celeste's attacks left and right, turns to Nona.

"Use the 'elemental rain' spell." Nona whispers into Luana's ear. Luana nods and whispers "elemental rain", and the elements – earth, rain, wind, and fire all rain down on the cottage, going through the fireplace and dousing the fire. The elements get to Celeste and batter her up. Celeste, taken by surprise, can barely dodge the elements, and, before long, she starts fighting back at Luana.

Back and forth, Luana and Celeste continue fighting, but, soon, Celeste begins to overpower Luana. Luana looks over at Nona irritably.

"You could help me, you know!" Luana exclaims.

Nona comes up beside Luana and takes out her sword, and begins blocking Celeste's attacks.

"Thanks."

"No problem."

Luana and Nona work together to dodge Celeste's attacks and fight back against her.

But, despite their best efforts, Luana's and Nona's energies drain as they keep fighting Celeste, and, shortly, Celeste overpowers the both of them, and Luana is struck down.

"Luana!" Nona drops her sword, and Celeste is taken by surprise by the clanging sword against the ground. The guards secure Celeste and tie her up so she can't use magic against anyone else.

"Luana?" Nona says again, holding Luana in her arms.

She's not waking up.

Luana starts suddenly glowing inside and out.

"Luana?"

"If she wakes up, I doubt she'll be normal." Celeste says.

"What's *that* supposed to mean?"

"It means that she'll no longer just be a royal; she'll also be a spell caster. Contrary to popular belief, I guess royals *and* spell casters can procreate."

Luana soon opens her eyes, and she looks at Nona. Luana has a golden aura around her, and she's actually glowing.

"Nona? What happened?"

"You're glowing, Luana. Literally."

Luana looks at herself.

"I guess I am."

"And you have magic. It'll be quite interesting to see and hear your explanation to your parents."

"Yeah...but I don't know how I'll explain it. No one in my family has magic. So, how do *I* have magic?"

"I don't know. All I know is, you're Gnypso's first royal spell caster."

"That sounds more like a job than a title."

"Same difference. The point is, Luana, I'll be there for you when you tell your parents that you have magic."

"Thank you, Nona." Nona nods at Luana before getting up and helping Luana up.

"Come on. Let's go home."

The group heads out and finds Emmitt still in the net.

"Emmitt!"

"Princess! I'm so glad you're safe!"

"Me, too, Emmitt."

Emmitt smiles.

"Now, can you help me down?"

"Yeah. Swing your feet down and you can stand on my shoulders. Richard," Nona starts, turning to the captain of the guard, "I need you to stand behind me and catch Emmitt."

"Of course, Nona."

Emmitt swings his feet down and Nona catches them, placing one on each of her shoulders.

"Okay, Emmitt. We've got you. You can let go of the net."

"I'm trusting you, Nona." Emmitt lets go and he stumbles back and Richard catches him and helps him stand up.

"There you go, son."

"Thank you."

"You're welcome. Now what, Nona?"

"Now, we go home."

"May I say something to Celeste first, please?"

"Of course, Emmitt." Richard says.

"Thanks. Nona, can you lead me over to her?"

"Yes, Emmitt."

Nona leads Emmitt over to Celeste.

"What could you possibly have to say to me, you traitor?"

"Celeste, I used to have a huge crush on you, but after experiencing the kindness and compassion my real friends gave me, and I changed, I don't have a crush on you anymore."

"You'll pay for this, Emmitt Northrup!" Celeste, her hands bound in front of her, throws an attack at Emmitt, but Luana blocks the attack.

"Surrender, Celeste. You have no other choice now." Luana demands.

"Fine, fine. I surrender. But I will have my revenge on you, Emmitt, for betraying me."

After securing Celeste on a horse, and with Luana riding with Richard and Emmitt riding with Nona, they all head back to Hartreusia, but not before heading to Hazel for her secret stew.

"Nona! Luana! Emmitt! It's so good to see you three again. And, Celeste! How are you, dear?"

"I've been better, Hazel. Considering I'm tied up against my will."

"Last time I checked, Celeste, *you* surrendered." Emmitt says, smirking at Celeste after finding her based on her voice.

"Details, details."

"Now, now, dears, it's time for you to have some of my secret stew." Hazel then notices the royal guard outside her door.

"Oh! I see you've brought some friends as well. Do come in, gentlemen, and have some of my secret stew."

"Uh, what's *in* the secret stew exactly?"

"Justin, Justin, Justin. If Hazel *told* you what was *in* her secret stew, it wouldn't be a *secret* stew, now would it?" Nona asks, semi-mocking Hazel's tone.

"A girl after my own heart!" Hazel exclaims before getting several bowls from her cabinet and distributing the stew into the bowls.

Everyone, including Celeste, eats the stew, and they thoroughly enjoy it.

After everyone eats their fill of the stew, and bidding farewell to Hazel, they mount their horses, and head to Hartreusia.

Once they reach Hartreusia, King Carter and Queen Juniper greet everyone at the front gates.

"Oh, thank the seven deities you're all safe and home!" Queen Juniper exclaims as Luana dismounts and approaches her parents. They hug their daughter tight, not willing to let her go again any time soon.

Isabella approaches Emmitt.

"Isa? Is that you?"

"It's me, Emmitt."

"Oh, thank the gods and goddesses you're safe, Isabella."

"How are you, Emmitt?"

"I'm fine. Just a bit frazzled from being almost killed by Celeste."

"She did *what*?!" Isabella walks up to Celeste.

"*This* is for nearly killing Emmitt!" Isabella punches Celeste in her jaw. She then turns away and heads back to Emmitt.

"Thank you for doing what I never could, Isa."

"You're welcome, Emmitt."

The king and queen beckon Nona over to them.

"Nona, we see you've delivered both Lady Isabella and Princess Luana safe and sound back home." King Carter observes.

"I have, Your Majesties."

"And, have you all become at least acquaintances?" Queen Juniper inquires.

"We have, Your Highness." Isabella says, stepping up with Emmitt on her arm.

"Queen Juniper and I are glad to hear it."

"Mum, Dad, there's something else you should know." Luana nervously says.

"What is it, Luana?" Queen Juniper asks.

"It's better if we do this in private, Mother." Luana says.

King Carter, Queen Juniper, Luana and Nona head inside to the king's chancery.

"What is this all about, sweetheart?" King Carter asks Luana.

"Well, Dad, it's pretty hard to explain, so, it's best if I just show you. Nona?"

Nona nods and takes a small statue of a peaswallow from the desk and places it in Luana's hands. Nona nods once again at Luana, signaling her to start.

"Sleight of Hand." Luana whispers into her palm. The statue shimmers, then disappears, and then reappears into Nona's outstretched hands.

"By the seven deities..." Queen Juniper gasps.

"How is this possible?" King Carter asks.

"I have no idea. It could be that some of the magic on Hazel's hut could have rubbed off on me. But I don't know that for sure."

"Still, it's remarkable. You're the first royal ever to be a spell caster." Queen Juniper says.

"Does anyone know about this magic?" King Carter asks.

"Celeste, Nona, the royal guard, and perhaps Emmitt."

"Who is Emmitt?"

"Emmitt helped us along the way. He used to be a friend of Celeste's." Luana immediately realizes she's said the wrong thing.

"He used to be a friend of the girl who held you hostage and who asked for a million zikapia for your ransom?" Queen Juniper asks.

"Yes, Mother."

"But he changed sides?"

"Yes, Mother."

"Very well. It seems he and Lady Isabella have gotten well acquainted."

"Yes. So much so that I feel it would be wrong to have a wedding between the two of you, Luana." King Carter states.

"Thank you, Father."

"You're welcome, Luana. It would not be wise to split the two of them, considering they've become so close over the past few days. It seems as though that you and Nona could perhaps marry after all. But, we'd rather you wait until we have returned from our trip to Indigonia."

"Yes, Father. We understand."

"Dismissed."

Luana turns to leave, but turns back.

"Father, may I speak with you for a moment?"

"Of course, Luana."

Nona leaves the room, and Luana walks up to her father.

"What is it, Lu?"

"I was wondering if Emmitt could maybe have a job shadowing under Hanna. He – he gouged his own eyes out so Celeste couldn't see where we were. He sacrificed his sight just so we could be safe."

"I don't see why not, Luana. But your mother and I expect you to introduce him to her."

"Yes, Father."

"Dismissed."

Luana leaves the room, and soon finds Emmitt on Isabella's arm, and they're talking to each other.

"Emmitt?"

"Yes, Princess?" Emmitt asks.

"May I introduce you to someone?"

"I'm not one to refuse royalty." Emmitt says, letting go of Isabella's arm and taking Luana's.

"I'll be back soon, m'lady." Emmitt states.

"I'll be waiting here, Emmitt."

Luana leads Emmitt to the kitchen and she spots Hanna.

"Hanna? I'd like to introduce you to someone."

"Yes, Princess?" Hanna walks up to Luana and Emmitt.

"This is Emmitt. He helped us along the way to Celeste."

"Ah, I thought I'd heard castle gossip about that girl. It's nice to meet you, Emmitt."

"You, too, Hanna. Princess Luana mentioned that you are the head baker here in Hartreusia's castle."

"I am."

"I myself love to bake all kinds of things, and I'd love to learn more."

"Then you've come to the right place, Emmitt. I'd be glad to teach you all I know about baking. Princess, you can leave him here with me so we can get started."

"Of course. Thank you again, Hanna."

"My pleasure, Princess."

"Oh, and Princess Luana?" Emmitt starts.

"Yes, Emmitt?"

"If you could send Lady Isabella our way, that would be fantastic."

"I will, Emmitt."

"Thanks."

Luana soon locates Isabella in the same place she and Emmitt left her and directs her to the kitchen to find Emmitt and Hanna.

~ Twelve ~

About a week later, Celeste's trial begins in front of the royal court. King Carter has hired a judge, Judge Francine, to preside the trial.

Emmitt, Luana, Isabella and Nona are all witnesses to Celeste's trial.

"All rise for Judge Francine."

The judge gets up to her stand and sits down.

"Be seated."

Everyone sits, and the lawyer for Celeste, Veronica, calls her first witness to the stand.

"I call my first witness, Emmitt Northrup, to the stand."

One of the royal guard escorts Emmitt to the witness stand, and he takes the oath to tell the truth.

"You may proceed to question the witness."

"Thank you, Your Honor. Mr. Northrup, is it true you and the defendant used to be close?"

"Yes, ma'am."

"Were you two friends?"

"Yes, ma'am, we were."

"And what caused the friendship to end?"

"Well, I was shown compassion and kindness by Princess Luana, Lady Isabella and Nona, and I was told that Celeste bullying me is not normal behavior."

"I see. So, would you say that my client was abusive towards you?"

"Yes, ma'am."

"Objection!" Celeste calls out.

"Overruled. Veronica, control your client."

"Yes, Your Honor. Celeste, calm yourself." Veronica turns back to Emmitt.

"Mr. Northrup, is it true that you gouged your own eyes out so Celeste would not be able to see where you were?"

"Yes, ma'am."

"And were you aware that, despite your best efforts, Celeste could still see all and know all through other people's eyes?"

"No, ma'am, I was not aware of that."

"No further questions, Your Honor."

"The witness may step down."

One of the royal guards escorts Emmitt back to his seat. Nona soon takes the stand as the next witness.

"Miss Hamlett, is it true that, at the age of four, you met Princess Luana and instantly became best friends?"

"Yes, that is correct."

"And is it true that my client had been ignored by both you and the princess that day?"

"Yes. But we didn't notice Celeste. We were only four years old at the time."

"I see. And is it true that my client secretly vowed revenge on both you and the princess for ignoring her?"

"As far as I know, that is true."

"No further questions."

"Call your next witness, counselor."

"I call Princess Luana Atteberry to the stand."

Luana takes the stand and takes the oath and is now being questioned by Celeste's lawyer.

"Your Highness, I understand that you have recently acquired magic, despite being born a royal."

"That is accurate."

"And how did you come upon having magic?"

"That I don't know because it just sort of burst out of me – literally."

"And your magic was used to help defeat my client?"

"Yes."

"Princess Luana, you were taken back to two moments in time by my client: one being the day of your horrible accident that gave you a permanent limp, and the other being the day you and Ms. Hamlett met."

"That is correct."

"And what did you see during those time trips?"

"Well, for the first one, I saw Nona and myself playing in one of the gardens on the palace grounds with my nanny and palace guards nearby. I saw Celeste in a tree, spying on us. Celeste moved a rock to trip me, and Celeste and Nona both shot out beams of magic, Celeste to let me fall, and Nona to catch me. Celeste's beam overpowered Nona's and I fell, which permanently damaged my leg."

"And what did you see during the second time trip, Your Highness?"

"I saw a younger version of Nona and myself talking to each other and I saw Celeste at the front of the crowd, looking longingly and jealously at Nona and myself. She wanted to be included, and I personally cannot fault her for that."

"But you can fault her for forever damaging your left leg, is that correct, Princess Luana?"

"I cannot fault her for something that was my own fault, but I *can* fault her for permanently causing a limp in my leg."

"Your Highness, I have but one more question for you: why did you ignore my client in your youth?"

"We were young children! I didn't ignore her knowingly. I didn't see her, and if I had, I'm sure I would have become friends with her as well."

"No further questions. I have one more witness to question, and then that will be all."

"The next witness may come up to the stand."

Isabella comes up and sits in the witness stand, ready to be questioned by Veronica.

"Your Ladyship, I presume you and Princess Luana were once engaged to each other, is that correct?"

"I don't see how that pertains to this case."

"Next question, counselor."

"Yes, Your Honor. Is it true that you and Mr. Northrup became infatuated with one another after he changed from being my client's pawn in her game of revenge?"

"Yes, that is correct."

"And is it true that you never got a full look at my client?"

"Mr. Northrup and I were taken by surprise by Celeste pulling a net out from under us."

"And is it true you abandoned Mr. Northrup, a blind man, to go get help?"

"He insisted I go get help, and he also insisted he would be fine for a while without me!"

"No further questions."

The court is dismissed until further notice.

A few weeks later, the jury has reached a verdict, and the witnesses, the lawyers, the rest of the court, and the defendant are all called back to hear the verdict.

"We find the defendant, Celeste Riker, guilty on all charges."

The room, minus Celeste and her lawyer, breathes a sigh of relief.

"Celeste is to be sentenced to the dungeon for the rest of her natural life. This case is now closed."

Celeste is escorted by the royal guard to the dungeon and Nona, Emmitt, Luana and Isabella all hug each other once they're all outside the courtroom.

"Lady Isabella?"

"Yes, Emmitt?"

"May I speak with you for a moment in private?"

"Of course."

King Carter and Queen Juniper invite Luana and Nona into the dining hall to have a celebratory drink.

"To Judge Francine! And the jury! And to justice!" King Carter exclaims, raising his glass.

"To justice!" Queen Juniper, Nona and Luana echo.

Suddenly, there are screams coming from the hallway.

"Luana, Nona, stay back. We'll deal with this." King Carter says. He and Queen Juniper head out into the hallway, and, soon after, King Carter pokes his head back into the dining hall.

"It's alright, Luana and Nona. You two might want to come see this." King Carter says, softly smiling at his daughter and Nona.

Luana and Nona follow King Carter out and they see, out in the garden, under one of the gazebos, Emmitt kneeling in front of Isabella.

"Oh, he's proposing!" Luana gasps.

Isabella nods and says yes to Emmitt's proposal. She helps him up and kisses him.

"How exciting! It looks like there might be a wedding after all!" Luana exclaims excitedly.

"Luana – that is, *Princess* Luana – may I speak to you for a moment?" Nona asks, taking Luana's hand.

"Of course, Nona."

The two head to a secluded area of the garden.

"Princess Luana, you and I have known each other for thirteen wonderful, yet hard, years. And, I've been wanting to ask you this for quite some time." Nona says before kneeling in front of Luana and taking her hand.

"Princess Luana Guinevere Atteberry, I love you so much, and I know I'm not royalty, but I don't care. Will you marry me?"

Luana develops tears in her eyes. Emmitt and Isabella wander over to them, keeping their distance, and Isabella whispers into Emmitt's ear what's going on.

"Yes, Nona! Yes, I will marry you!" Nona gets up and kisses Luana.

Emmitt and Isabella go over to Nona and Luana and embrace them.

"I believe congratulations are in order." Emmitt says.

"For all of us, Emmitt. We couldn't have made it through this journey without you. Thank you." Luana says, hugging Emmitt.

"You're welcome, Princess."

The hug soon breaks.

"Come on. Let's go make the royal announcements." Luana says, arm in arm with Nona.

Isabella offers Emmitt her elbow, and he takes it. They head back into the castle. After a brief chat with Isabella's parents, and Luana's parents, the two royal couples head out to the balcony to await the oncoming crowd.

"Presenting, Her Ladyship, Isabella Villareal of Rosiary, and Emmitt Northrup of Lavenderia, and Her Royal Highness, Princess Luana Atteberry of Hartreusia, and Nona Hamlett of Rosiary. Let us all congratulate them on their respective engagements!"

The crowd cheers and throws flowers while the two couples wave gracefully to the crowd.

"I guess this means there will be two royal weddings instead of just one." Queen Juniper remarks to King Carter.

"I guess there will be, Juniper."

After the announcement of the royal engagements, royal wedding preparations begin to get underway.

Luana will be coronated as queen after the wedding, and, afterwards, her parents will step down to begin an early retirement.

The two royal couples make their separate guest lists, and it's decided to have a double royal wedding instead of two separate ones, considering Hazel, Holly and Julia are on both lists.

After the guest list has been approved, Luana and Isabella are with the royal dressmakers, while Nona and Emmitt are with two of the other royal dressmakers in a separate wing of the castle, so that the surprise of the royal brides' ensembles won't be spoiled for their future spouses.

Luana will be wearing an off-the-shoulder ball gown with a gold and white bodice, sweetheart neckline, and gold details on the white skirt, a chapel train and a cathedral veil, while Isabella will be wearing a lace ball gown with long sleeves, a sweetheart neckline, and a sweep train and walking veil.

Nona will be wearing a simple white lace gown that has a scoop neckline, sweep train and a fingertip veil, while Emmitt will be wearing a white uniform with blue details, as it is Isabella's favorite color.

Hanna, one of the top royal bakers in the kingdom, will be making the wedding cakes for the royal couples. Her assistant, Beatrice, places samples of cake on the table before the royal couples, so they can taste them and see which ones they like the most for their respective cakes. Emmitt and Isabella go through seven flavors, while Luana and Nona go through five.

Emmitt and Isabella taste the first flavor, a lemon raspberry sponge cake with raspberry filling and a white chocolate buttercream. They go on tasting the six other flavors, but the lemon raspberry sponge is their favorite. Luana and Nona taste their first flavor, a chocolate cake with a caramel filling and milk chocolate ganache as the frosting. They continue tasting the four other flavors, but the chocolate cake is their favorite.

Now that the respective cake flavors have been chosen, next is choosing the venue.

"It would make sense to have it in the royal chapel." Emmitt says.

"That *would* be the best place for us to get married. And it makes the best sense." Luana says.

"It's settled then; we'll get married in the Royal Chapel of the Seven Deities." Isabella says.

The royal couples decide that Holly, Julia and Hazel can cater their double wedding with Hazel's Secret Stew, and Holly and Julia's mead and beer. The rest of the castle's kitchen staff will do the remainder of the catering.

The royal couples send out save-the-date cards, and everyone RSVP's as soon as they can, all of the answers being positive. The guest list is at one thousand guests, and that's the limit of the royal chapel.

"I guess we don't need to register for anything, as m'lady and I will be moving back to the manor in Rosiary after the wedding."

"Oh, do say that you two will visit often." Luana begs.

"We'll visit as much as we can." Emmitt promises.

The florals are chosen next: a bouquet of lilies for Isabella, roses for Luana and blue hydrangeas for Nona. The two couples hire royal musicians to play at their wedding, and the playlists for the wedding are compared and shortened so they don't conflict with each other. After that is all done, the officiant is hired for the couples.

The rings are then chosen: a gold band for Emmitt, a simple golden ring with a halo of diamonds for Isabella, a princess-cut diamond ring for Luana and a baguette-cut diamond ring for Nona. Hair and makeup trials are next, and Luana goes for a simple braided updo for her scarlet hair, while Nona chooses two small braids going around the sides and the back of her head for her brown hair, and Isabella chooses simple curls for her black hair. Each of the young ladies chooses a simple makeup look.

Luana and Isabella go together to a secluded part of the library to write their vows to their own future spouses, while Nona and Emmitt do the same. They've decided to have a bit of a religious aspect to the ceremony.

Centerpieces of flameless candles in vases with stones are made, final decisions are completed, and, thereafter, the double royal wedding is fast approaching.

There is peace in all the lands, but the story is not quite over yet.

~ Thirteen ~

A few weeks have passed since wedding planning began, and Emmitt is being escorted down to the dungeons, not because he's done anything wrong, but because he wants to visit his ex-best friend and ex-crush, Celeste.

"Richard, can you give us a few minutes alone, please?"

"Of course, Emmitt. I'll be just outside the door."

"Thank you."

"Emmitt. My dear old friend. Have you come to see me?"

"Yes, but this isn't a social call. I want some answers, Celeste."

"Oh? And what questions could you possibly have for me?"

"Well, for starters, I want to know why you treated me so badly."

"Well, as they say, hurt people hurt people. Come now, Emmitt. You should be glad I didn't treat you worse."

"Glad you didn't treat me *worse*? Celeste, you treated me terribly! You couldn't have treated me worse!"

"Tut, tut. And to think we used to be good friends."

"Operative words being 'used to'."

"Is that all you came down here to ask me?"

"No. I have more questions."

"Go on, then. Ask away."

"Fine. Is it true you can really see all, even if you can't see through my eyes anymore?"

"Yes. Next question."

"I know why you hurt Princess Luana, but did you have to give her a permanent limp?"

"It's because she ignored me when she and I were young."

"And you think that causing a permanent limp in someone is a good solution to that?"

"Why do you care?"

"Princess Luana is my best friend."

"If she was *really* your best friend, she would've been able to heal your eyes...or lack thereof."

"I don't need to see. I have my four other senses. I can tell you're being bitter by the sound of your voice, Celeste. You just want me on your side again, don't you? Well, it won't work."

"Oh, Emmitt. Emmitt, Emmitt, Emmitt. Don't you get it? I was your first real friend that wasn't family. If it weren't for me, you would've died in the fire I set on your house."

"Wait a second, you did *what*? *You* were the one that set my house on fire? I lost my parents and most of my siblings because of you! I should've known you were trouble when I first laid eyes on you. And another thing, you should consider yourself lucky that you're behind bars, Celeste, because if you weren't, I'd unleash hell upon you for killing, no, *murdering*, my family!"

"You poor, poor thing. Rendered blind by his own actions, and the only family remaining is his little fiancée, and her family. Poor, poor, *poor* Emmitt."

"I don't really care that I'm blind. But what I *do* care about is if you hurt my Isabella or my in-laws. They've hurt enough after they lost Dawn."

"Awww, boo-hoo. You listen to me, Emmitt Northrup, nice and clear. One day I will escape from this prison, and I *will* exact my revenge on your found family for putting me behind bars."

"Is that a threat?"

"No. It's a promise. Emmitt, I can tell you one thing: if you let me out of this birdcage, I can promise you I won't hurt you or your little chosen family. But if you don't, you'll be sorry. I'll make *sure* of it." Celeste says.

Emmitt steps back, astonished at Celeste's threat towards his found family.

"Guard!"

Richard comes back in and appears at Emmitt's side.

"Yes, Emmitt?"

"I'd like to leave now, please. I must inform the king and queen of what Celeste has just told me."

"Right away." Richard leads Emmitt up the stairs and helps him walk to the king's office, where King Carter and Queen Juniper are.

"Emmitt? Is there something the matter?" Queen Juniper asks.

"Yes, Your Majesty, there is."

Emmitt begins to explain his conversation with Celeste, telling the king and queen the threats she had made against him, and his found family.

"Your Majesties? Pardon the interruption, but you wanted to see me?" The three in the king's office turn to find Matilde, the leader of the Dangerous Deviants, in the doorway.

"Matilde?"

"Emmitt? What are you doing here?"

"Didn't you hear, sis? I'm getting married to Lady Isabella of Rosiary."

"I meant, what are you doing *here*, in His Majesty's office?"

"Oh. I came to tell Their Majesties about the threats Celeste made against me and my found family."

"Emmitt, why are you wearing sunglasses indoors?" Matilde asks of her younger brother.

"Well, you see, sis, I – I gouged my eyes out so Celeste wouldn't be able to see what I was doing or where I was."

"You did *what*?"

"Because of what Celeste has put me through over the years, and because of the kindness and compassion Nona, Princess Luana and Lady Isabella all showed me over the course of a week, I feel like I owed it to them to not let Celeste know where we were. After all, I don't believe that Celeste has ever been a good person. She *was* the girl who caused Luana's permanent limp."

King Carter stands up, pushing back his chair.

"*Celeste* was the girl who caused my little girl's limp? Not Nona?"

"While Princess Luana was being held hostage by Celeste, I was in a net in front of the door, and I could hear their conversation, and, from what we heard at the trial, Celeste took herself and Princess Luana back to the day of the accident."

"How?"

"By magic. *Dark* magic."

"I thought dark magic was just a myth." Queen Juniper says.

"It's not, Your Highness. I've seen Celeste do terrible things, and each time I tried to go to tell her off or tell someone about what she's done, she wiped my memory of the event of her terrible deeds. It's like she knew what I was about to do." Emmitt remarks.

"Luana mentioned something about her knowing all and seeing all. Do you think that could be connected to her dark magic?" King Carter inquires.

"I'm most certain that it could be, King Carter."

"And is there any possible chance that Luana could be affected with the dark magic?"

"I wouldn't say no to that. It *is* possible, Your Majesty."

"And how do we tell if Celeste has infected my daughter with dark magic?"

"I'm not entirely sure. I, like you, thought dark magic was a myth until I heard Princess Luana talking about what she saw during the time trips."

"You've hung around Celeste for almost a decade, and you didn't see anything about dark magic?"

"N-no, Your Majesty." Emmitt says, nervously backing up.

"Carter, you're scaring him." Queen Juniper tells her husband.

"I'm sorry for scaring you, son. I'm just trying to get some answers here."

"Celeste would be the one you want to talk to then, Your Majesty. She's the one with the answers."

"We'll interrogate her at once. Matilde?"

"Yes, sire?"

"I need you to accompany your brother back to his room."

"Yes, Your Majesty. Come on, Emmitt."

Emmitt and Matilde walk back to Emmitt's room while King Carter and Queen Juniper go down to the dungeon to interrogate Celeste on her dark magic.

"Richard, we're here to interrogate Celeste."

"She told me she won't talk without her lawyer present."

"Very well. Fetch her lawyer, then we'll get the answers we need."

Soon after, Celeste, her lawyer Veronica, King Carter and Queen Juniper are sitting down at a table, ready to interrogate Celeste.

"Celeste, is it true you used dark magic on Princess Luana to take her back to the day of the accident, and to the day that she and Nona met?"

"What's it to you?"

"I need to know whether *your dark magic* has affected my Luana!"

"If it has, it's because her new magic has taken over her bloodstream, and my dark magic is a part of her new magic. Put it this way, Carter, can I call you Carter?"

"No, you may not!"

"Anyway, once I kickstarted your daughter's magic by showing her the past, some of my magic must've flowed through her, giving *her* magic, too. Who knows if my dark magic will affect her? I sure don't."

"We're getting nowhere." Queen Juniper whispers to King Carter.

"It's best if we just go, Juniper. We've got a rehearsal ball to plan." King Carter whispers back.

"Oh, yes. Go and plan your little rehearsal ball. It's not as if your daughter's *life* is at stake. But go on, enjoy your party."

King Carter glowers as the cell door closes behind him and Queen Juniper.

"Dear, we *do* have a party to plan. Come on, and let's enjoy the time we have with our daughter, no matter how short that time may be."

~.~

A few months have passed since the interrogation, and it is time for the rehearsal ball for the double royal wedding.

When the party guests arrive, they know that this is the party of the century and should be treated as such.

"Please, everyone, take your seats. The rehearsal ball is about to begin, and once the royal brides enter after Emmitt and Nona enter, please stand. Once I say to sit, please be seated. I will say a few words, honoring the seven gods and goddesses, and then the couples will begin their vows, exchange their rings, and seal their respective marriages with a kiss. Rice will be thrown to the happy couples and we will proceed to the reception." The officiant, Judge Francine, says.

Everyone murmurs in agreement.

As the music starts, Emmitt and Nona enter the chapel, dressed in simple ensembles, yet formal enough for the rehearsal ball.

Everyone stands as the two brides enter the chapel, both escorted by their own fathers.

The brides make it to the end of the aisle, and both Luana and Isabella kiss their fathers on the cheek, as they would tomorrow.

"Be seated, folks. I say something along the lines of 'we are here to celebrate the marriages of these two wonderful couples, and it was not an easy feat to get here to this day' and I continue on my spiel, they say their vows, exchange the rings, and seal their respective marriage with a kiss."

There's suddenly slow clapping coming from the back.

"And, before all of that, you ask if anyone objects to the marriage. Because *I* sure do."

"It's Celeste! Who let her in here? I demand to know who let Celeste in here!" King Carter bellows.

"Oh, don't bother. I let *myself* in here. Let's see, I knocked out your top guard, escaped the dungeon, dodged the rest of the royal guard, and made it in here," Celeste says, counting off on her fingers, "You think I'm going to come quietly, or surrender like I did before? You've got the wrong girl this time. I intend to exact my revenge on your daughter, Emmitt, Nona, and, why not throw Lady Isabella into the mix? I'll exact my revenge on all four of them. But, first, I'll give out my revenge on the one person I thought I could count on: Emmitt Northrup."

"Not if we have any say in it!" Isabella steps forward, taking her bow and quiver of arrows from her mother.

Luana and Nona step forward, all three girls surrounding Emmitt. Celeste whispers into her palm and a bolt of lightning shoots out from the sky through the chapel roof and almost hits Emmitt, but Isabella knocks him out of the way in time.

"Isabella, get everyone out of here, including yourself and Emmitt! We'll take care of Celeste." Luana says.

"Be careful." Isabella says.

"When have we not been?" Nona and Luana say, joining hands as their magic connects together.

"There is no way we're letting this girl take hold of these young people's special day!" One of the guests exclaims.

~ Fourteen ~

The guests join together in a linked-arm line around Emmitt as Luana, Nona and Isabella stand at the front of the crowd, Luana and Nona with their magic, and Isabella with her bow and quiver of arrows. Isabella nocks an arrow and aims it at Celeste.

"Luana, we all know that you're a novice at magic. There's *no way* you could have a hand in my defeat." Celeste says.

Hazel suddenly comes in, pushing the door and Celeste out of the way.

"I'm sorry I'm late, peoples! I had to make sure that my secret stew was ready for tomorrow!"

It's then Hazel notices Celeste behind the door, almost squished.

"Oh, Celeste, dearie. I thought you were in the dungeon."

"I escaped, you old crone."

"Are you causing trouble for these nice young people?" Hazel asks, her hands on her hips.

"They were the reason I was in the dungeon!"

"That doesn't excuse your behavior, Celeste Elizabeth Riker!" Hazel exclaims.

Hazel backs up towards Luana, Nona and Isabella, puts her hands together and stretches them out, revealing her own magic.

"Hazel, we didn't think you *had* magic!" Nona cries.

"I've been saving it up over the years, girlie. This old gal has magic to boot!"

"You really think a princess, a spell caster, a girl with a bow and arrow and an old crone can defeat me?"

"We *know* we can defeat you, Celeste."

"Go ahead and try. But I can guarantee that you will rue this – "

Isabella shoots an arrow at Celeste's sleeves, pinning it to the back wall. Celeste simply rips her sleeve out from the arrow.

Celeste gathers up her magic and begins to fight back with different spells left and right, but, with the spell casters, commoners and royals all fighting back, Celeste is eventually defeated, and the guards return Celeste into custody.

"Any last words before you're taken back to the dungeon where you belong?" Luana asks.

"Just a few, *Princess*. You will rue this day. You will *all* rue this day!"

The guards take Celeste away to the dungeon, and the rehearsal ball resumes.

During the dinner portion of the rehearsal, King Carter raises his goblet to make a mini-toast in preparation for his real toast the following day.

"It is tradition that the story of the founding of Planet Gnypso be told on each birthday, wedding, and funeral of the royal families. The real version I will tell tomorrow, but the gist of it is that the end of the world was upon my ancestors, and, in the year 2864, they left Planet Earth for this planet, and the royals each founded their own countries, the Atteberrys founded Hartreusia, the Morrisons founded Eburnean, the Cantrells founded Indigonia, the Arellanos founded Lavenderia, and the Villareals founded Rosiary. They came together to form a new world, and they promised peace throughout all the lands. I will also say something quite embarrassing for my daughter, Princess Luana, as is custom as her father, and welcome our new daughter-in-law and queen consort into the family, and into the kingdom."

"And I will make a speech embarrassing my own daughter, Lady Isabella." Lord Dustin says, chuckling. The guests chuckle in response.

"The festivities will continue throughout the night, and end with the double-send-off of the royal couples. The coronation of Princess Luana into *Queen* Luana will take place in a week's time from the double royal wedding. As for now, enjoy the feast and yourselves, and thank you all for attending my daughter's rehearsal ball and wedding."

Nona and Luana sneak away to the library after the rehearsal ball with Emmitt and Isabella, ready to swap stories with each other.

"Did we ever tell you guys about how Luana and I met?" Nona inquires.

"No, you did not." Emmitt remarks.

"Well, it's about time we tell you how Princess Luana and I met. We were four at the time, and King Carter and Queen Juniper and Luana were visiting Rosiary to see how the commoners were fairing after the big storm that had hit us. Despite the repairs that needed to be made to our small village, my parents and I went to see the royals, and Luana and I locked eyes, and it was an instant connection, and an instant friendship."

"Little did I know that Celeste was in the crowd, looking longingly and jealously at Nona and me. She was plotting revenge against us, because we didn't include her."

"That's why she hates you." Emmitt remarks.

"That's exactly why. I wish I could make amends with her."

"I believe it's too late for that now, Luana. Shall we get on with the tale?"

"Yes. Over time, Nona's and my friendship grew, and it blossomed into something more – a romance."

"But, alas, it was not to be. For royals and spell casters could not marry at the time, and it was forbidden for even nonspellers and spell casters to marry."

"But that all changed with a red-haired princess and a brown-haired spell caster about, say, thirteen years after your meeting?" Emmitt says.

"Exactly. Nona and I have made history as the first princess and spell caster to ever marry. Well, as of tomorrow, anyway."

"It's time I tell you all how Celeste and I met, and how my parents and all but one of my siblings died. I was eight at the time, as was Celeste. I was playing ball with my siblings when I noticed Celeste practicing the 'sleight of hand' spell."

~.~

Emmitt is walking by when he notices Celeste practicing the spell.

"Whoa! That's really cool! You're a spell caster?" Emmitt asks.

"Yep! Only two more years until I can really use my magic!"

One of Emmitt's siblings accidentally kicks a ball into Celeste's backyard.

"Could we have our ball back, please?" Emmitt asks.

"Sure!" But instead of just simply throwing it back, Celeste decides to use the "sleight of hand" spell. She says the spell by closing her eyes and whispering the spell into her hands that are holding the ball, and the ball shimmers, disappears and then reappears into the little boy's hands.

"That's so cool. What's your name?"

"Celeste. What's your name?"

"Emmitt. Do you want to be best friends forever?"

"Yes!"

Emmitt and Celeste hug and they begin playing with Emmitt's siblings.

A few days pass, and Celeste and Emmitt are out playing in Emmitt's backyard while Celeste's grandmother and Emmitt's grandparents are out shopping.

Suddenly, screams come from inside Emmitt's house, and Celeste and Emmitt stop their playing.

They turn, and see Emmitt's house ablaze!

"What do we do?" Emmitt asks Celeste.

"I don't know, Emmitt."

The fire department comes and douses the fire, but it's too late for Emmitt's parents, brothers and sisters.

"Emmitt!" Emmitt and Celeste go towards the voice, and it's one of the firefighters.

"Emmitt...we were too late to save your parents and siblings. We're so sorry for your loss."

"My mummy, daddy, and all my brothers and sisters are gone?"

"We're afraid so, son. But your grandparents are here to take care of you. You're going to live with them now. Celeste, we'll take you back to your grandmother."

"Okay. Thank you." Celeste says.

Emmitt is in complete shock as he's being led to his grandparents.

Celeste and Emmitt say their goodbyes, and Emmitt goes home to his grandparents' house, and Celeste heads back to Lavenderia to stay with her grandmother.

After seven more years pass from that day, Emmitt was doing the grocery shopping for his grandparents. While getting the things needed for the week, Emmitt's grandparents are killed by rabid elves, and, at fifteen, Emmitt is left alone.

When Emmitt walks through the front door of his grandparents' house, he finds them dead on the floor, surrounded by dead rabid elves. With nothing but the clothes on his back and the groceries, Emmitt travels to Lavenderia, and he moves in with Celeste and her grandmother until he has enough money to move out on his own a couple of years later.

"And that's the story of how I met Celeste, how I lost my parents and most of my siblings, and how I lost my grandparents."

"Oh, Emmitt. We're so sorry you went through that." Luana apologizes.

"Thank you, Luana. It means a lot to me."

"It's getting pretty late, and we have to get up early tomorrow." Isabella says.

"That we do." Luana says.

The four friends get up, hug, and head their separate ways for the night, Isabella to her guest suite, Nona to her place in the servants' quarters (for the last time), Emmitt to his guest suite (escorted by Richard, the head guard), and Luana to her bedchamber.

~ Fifteen ~

Luana wakes up to find Isla and her other maids looking at her with smiles on their faces.

"Princess, it's time to get you ready for your wedding day! The royal dressmaker just dropped off your gown, and, I must say, Your Highness, that it is absolutely beautiful." Isla says.

"Thank you, Isla."

"You're welcome. Come, let's get you bathed and dressed for your big day."

There's suddenly a knock at the door.

"I'll get it." Olivia, one of Luana's maids, remarks. She walks over to the double doors and opens them.

"Your Majesty!" Olivia and the other maids immediately go into a curtsy as Queen Juniper enters the room.

"I just came to see how my daughter and future queen is faring."

"I'm fine, Mum. Just anxious, and a little bit nervous for the upcoming wedding."

"Oh, of course you're nervous! I was, too, when I was about to marry your father. Come, let me help you get ready."

"Mother, I'm sure my ladies' maids can assist me with getting ready for today."

Queen Juniper sighs, then nods.

"Very well. But I will be performing an inspection with you before you enter the chapel."

"Yes, Mother."

Queen Juniper leaves and Luana's ladies' maids help Luana bathe and dress for the wedding. Her red hair is in a tight braided bun, and a bridal tiara is placed on her head with her cathedral veil. Her shoes are simple white flats.

"Well, girls, how do I look in my wedding dress?" Luana asks.

"You look absolutely beautiful, Princess. Nona is going to love you more than she already does."

"Thank you, Olivia."

"Well, we'd better go attend to Nona and help *her* get ready. Would you like one of us to wait with you?"

"I'll be fine, Isla."

"Very well, Your Highness. We'll see you at the altar."

Meanwhile, Nona is pacing back and forth in her bedroom, ready to get this show on the road.

"Nona? Are you ready to get ready?" Isla asks.

"I am, Isla."

Nona's coworkers help Nona bathe and get into her wedding dress, shoes and veil.

"Do you think my attire pretty enough for a future queen consort?" Nona asks.

"It's absolutely beautiful, and it's *perfect* for a future queen consort."

"Thank you, Isla. How is my bride-to-be doing, by the way?"

"She's doing just fine, Nona. She's going to love you more than she already does."

"Thank you."

In another part of the castle, Emmitt is getting ready on his own, with King Carter's supervision.

"Well, Your Majesty? How do I look?" Emmitt asks. Emmitt is wearing a white uniform with blue details.

"You look very handsome, son. Lady Isabella will fall all the more in love with you."

"Thank you, King Carter. It means a lot to me that you're here for me."

"You're quite welcome. I'd better go see if my little girl is almost ready for her entrance. Will you be alright on your own for a while?"

"Yes, King Carter. I'll be just fine."

"That's good to hear."

In yet another part of the castle, Isabella is getting ready with her own ladies' maids.

"You look absolutely beautiful, Lady Isabella. Mr. Northrup will love it and you, Your Ladyship!"

"Thank you, Amalie."

"You're welcome."

Around the castle, the morning bells are heard to signal the start of the day.

"Well, we'd better get to the chapel." Isabella says.

Soon, Nona and Emmitt meet to walk to the chapel together, to wait for their brides.

The music starts, and Nona and Emmitt walk arm-in-arm to the end of the aisle. Richard is there to describe Isabella's look to Emmitt once she enters with her father.

The bridal entrance music starts, the guests stand for the presentation of the brides, and Isabella walks down the aisle with her parents, Lord Dustin and Lady Alissa, and, behind them, Luana walks down the aisle with her parents, King Carter and Queen Juniper.

Soon, the two couples meet at the end of the aisle.

"Be seated. Welcome to the royal wedding of Lady Isabella Villareal and Emmitt Northrup, and the royal wedding of Princess Luana Atteberry and Nona Hamlett. Now, before we begin with the prayer to the gods and goddesses of Destiny, does anyone object to these unions?" The officiant inquires.

Thankfully, no one objects.

"We will now begin with the prayer to the gods and goddesses of Destiny. I'm sure the deities will make an exception for us not kneeling, since most of you are in gowns. Let us pray. Oh, Aileen, goddess of all humans and creatures; Nellie, goddess of healing; Erik, god of magic; Irah, god of nature; Loana, goddess of wisdom; Era, goddess of time; and Sena, goddess of beauty; I pray to you yesterday, today, tomorrow and forever to watch over and be with Lady Isabella Villareal, Emmitt Northrup, Princess Luana Atteberry, and Nona Hamlett, as they journey forth from this day as married couples.

"Please show them that beauty is not only on the outside, but also on the inside. Give them wisdom, to manage their time wisely, to love each other in sickness and in health, to guide Princess Luana and Nona as they use their magic throughout life, and to help guide them through the forests of uncertainty. By the power of the seven deities, so be it."

"So be it." The voices echo around the officiant.

"Now, Princess Luana, you and Nona may begin your vows."

"Nona, my dear, sweet Nona, from the moment we met, I knew you were someone special, and I had a strong feeling that our bond would eventually be something more than friendship. So, today, in front of our families and friends, I, Luana Guinevere Atteberry, take you, Nona June Hamlett, to be my wife. Through all the times and trials, through friendship and romance, we will be joined as one."

"Luana, my princess, my darling, my everything, I love you more than life itself. So, I, Nona June Hamlett, in front of our families and friends, take you, Luana Guinevere Atteberry, to be my wife. Through all the times and trials, through friendship and romance, we will be joined as one."

"Lady Isabella, you and Emmitt may begin your vows."

"Emmitt, my goofball, my friend, my love. When we met, I didn't know that you and I would become friends, and I certainly didn't know that we would become each other's true love. I love you yesterday, today, tomorrow and forever, and I, Isabella Delilah Villareal, take you, Emmitt James Northrup, to be my husband. Through all the times and trials, through friendship and romance, we will be joined as one."

"Isabella, my sweetheart, my gorgeous, gorgeous girl, I love you with my entire being. I, too, didn't know that we'd become friends and, eventually, betrothed. I love you yesterday, today, tomorrow, and forever, and I, Emmitt James Northrup, take you, Isabella Delilah Villareal, to be my wife. Through all times and trials, through friendship and romance, we will be joined as one."

The rings are then exchanged between the couples.

"By the power vested in me, by the seven deities and by the country of Hartreusia, I now pronounce you married. You may seal your marriage with a kiss."

Nona and Luana kiss each other, and Isabella and Emmitt kiss each other.

"I am proud to announce for the very first time, Mr. and Mrs. Emmitt James Northrup, and Mrs. Luana and Mrs. Nona Atteberry."

The applause is nearly deafening as the couples walk back down the aisle.

The reception is magnificent, and, when the royal couples enter, the ballroom is filled with tables and food and two wedding cakes. The wedding cakes are both white, and one has blue flowers, for Isabella and Emmitt, and the other has red flowers, for Luana and Nona.

Luana and Nona dance to their song, and then Isabella and Emmitt dance to their song.

The feast begins, the couples mingle with their guests, and the dancing, although embarrassing at times, is nice.

The party is grand. There's laughter, fun and games, dancing, music, and lots of food eaten by the guests and the royal couples.

Soon, the King stands for his speech.

"I want to thank you all for coming to my daughter's wedding. Now, it's time for the speech you have all been waiting for. The year is 2864, and there is complete chaos. It's the literal end of the world, and my great-grandfather, King Graham Atteberry, left with his wife, Queen Anne Lupton, and his people, to the dwarf planet Gnypso we now call home. On September 25, 2865, Gnypso was founded, along with the five countries, each a play on a color, Hartreusia for chartreuse, Rosiary for rose, Indigonia for indigo, Eburnean for eburnean, and Lavenderia for lavender. Two years later King Graham and Queen Anne welcomed Shamus, my grandfather, into the world, and he later married Lucille Fitzcharles, who had a son, my father, named Emerson.

"Emerson later married Dianna Carlton and they had me, Carter Atteberry, who later married Juniper Altman. We later had a daughter named Luana. Our Luana's birth was the happiest day of our lives, and she had many firsts, as all babies do. But I believe my favorite of those firsts was her first word. I'll never forget her first word, which was 'dada'."

The guests chuckle as they imagine the princess' first word.

More speeches are made, and the festivities continue throughout the night.

However, there is one person who is not in attendance:

Celeste.

She is currently on a horse, galloping through the gates of the castle, away from Hartreusia, back to Lavenderia.

She doesn't stop for anything, not for food, not for water, not for sleep.

As she stops at her cottage, she lowers the hood of her cloak, walks into her cottage, and goes to a back room, hearing crying.

She approaches the crib, and picks up the crying baby girl.

"Don't worry, my little one. I will make sure your father pays for leaving me. Leaving us. And I *will* get revenge on that precious princess of Hartreusia. She's the reason you nearly starved." Going to the window with her daughter, Celeste looks out on the world, swearing revenge on all those who have hurt her and, unknowingly, her daughter.